WIRE: A WINGS OF DIABLO MC NOVEL

RAE B. LAKE

ACKNOWLEDGMENTS

Special Thanks!
To My Babe, I would never have been able to complete any of my
books without your support. Thank you for everything you do, day in
and out!
To Princess, I love you more and more each day.
To my fans, friends, and family. Thank you from the bottom of my
heart for all the support and kind words.

CHAPTER

Wire

Shit! I grabbed my side and hobbled as fast as I could towards the alley.

"Don't run now, motherfucker!" The roar of the metal beasts choked off as they came to a stop closer to me than I would have liked.

I was stuck - up shit creek - in a bad way, whatever you wanted to call it. Here I was running through the back alleys of an affluent neighborhood, my blood smearing all over the laundry hanging in the back yards. I stayed close to the shadows, my sweat the only thing blurring my vision.

I pressed down on the wound in my side; it was bleeding like a bitch. I knew that if I didn't get help soon, I was bound to pass out, leaving me completely helpless at the hands of the Tears of Chaos. They had been our rival club since before I was even a patched member. And since I'd been patched, we've done some shit that'd caused serious bodily harm to a shit ton of their members, mostly by my hand. Today that was coming back to bite me in the ass.

"Where the fuck are you?" Monte called out from somewhere nearby.

I could take him one on one but with my injury, it would take me longer than it usually would and his goons would have the chance to surround me. That plan wouldn't work. I pulled out my 9mm Taurus, all silver and gleaming in the moonlight. I'd already popped off close to a dozen rounds, as I tried to get the bastards off my tail, but I had only made contact with one shot and it had done nothing to slow them down. I had two rounds left and one in the chamber. Firing randomly was getting me nowhere.

The ground suddenly tilted upwards and I could feel my body about to go down. I was losing too much blood. I slammed my head back, hitting the windowpane of the house I was cowering against. The window rattled but it didn't break. *Thank God for small miracles.*

"What the fuck was that?"

"It came from over there!"

Footsteps, loud and determined, were coming in my direction. I looked around, trying to find my next avenue of escape. A wooden plank fence encased the yard as tall as my head, and in the shape that I was in, there was no way that I was going to be able to climb it. Looking down the other side alley, I saw Farmer; his fat ass was already huffing his way down the alley towards me. His legs looked like trembling toothpicks holding up his rotund upper body. He was so fat; I'd heard they had to have his kutte custom made using the same amount of leather it would've taken to make four normal size pieces. The man was massive and slow to boot. I had never understood why they kept that liability on the road.

Either way, I was never going to make it past him.

"Watch when I get my hands on you, boy! You're gonna wish you'd never crossed me, that you never crossed Chaos," Monte screamed out, swiping at towels that were hanging on someone's laundry line.

I huffed out my breath; there was no way out. I banged my head back in frustration. *Fuck it.* If this was going to be my end, then I was taking these dirtbags out right along with me. I sucked in a big breath, ready to make my location known. *Let them come to me.* I stepped off the wall and steadied my hand to shoot at the first sign of anyone coming around the corner. I was hoping it was Monte; I would love to take him out.

A light flashed to my right. I turned, my gun quickly drawn straight up.

Gold simmering eyes, staring straight into the barrel of my gun, tears threatening to run down her cheeks. Her chest was heaving; she was getting ready to scream.

Quickly I lowered my gun and put a finger to my mouth, hoping with everything I was, she wouldn't scream.

Her mouth snapped shut. But her eyes went straight to the 9mm in my hand.

"Wire! I can smell you. Just wait until I find your ass!" Monte screamed out again. He seemed to be all around me yet not close enough to see me.

Both of our heads turned around when Monte screamed out. I turned back towards her as she turned her head to face me. Her eyes scanned my body, trying to assess how much of a threat I was to her. The river of blood pouring down my pants must have signified that I wasn't going to kill her right then because she stepped back into her house, waving me inside. The woman was a fucking angel. I hurried in as quietly as I could.

As I entered the house, she called out softly, "Max." She looked past me, waiting for this Max person. *Great!* All I needed was more fucking witnesses.

I almost laughed out loud when a huge pile of hair came trotting up towards her. Max was a golden retriever and a huge one at that. I was sure that if he stood up on his hind legs, we would be the same height and I was not a little dude by any means, *anywhere.*

She opened the door again. "Protect the house, boy." He trotted out to the back yard where I'd just been hiding. The woman was a goddamn genius.

She closed the door, slowly turning her back to me and watched out the small slit in her blinds. She was biting her nails. She must have been worried about the dog because she had a bloodied stranger right next to her and she didn't even pay me any mind.

"Hey," I whispered in her direction.

"Shhh!" She glared at me, rolling her eyes, she turned her attention back to her dog.

A low growl emanated from the back yard and Max stood up. Front legs bent a bit, hind legs taut with readiness.

"Fuck." I could see Monte with his gun drawn, staring at the large dog that looked as if he was going to rip him to shreds. "That twat isn't back here." He called out behind him.

"Man, are you sure. I could have sworn the sounds came from around here," another one of his henchmen called out from somewhere near the front of the house.

"Yes. I'm sure. I mean, unless you want to try your luck against this beast of a mutt back here!" Monte spat out.

I heard him rustle around and Max sat back down in the middle of the yard like nothing had ever happened, rubbing his muzzle into a pile of dirt then rubbing it off with his massive paw. The clock hand ticked on by as I practically held my breath, waiting for the next shoe to drop. When I heard the roar of four motorcycle engines and one three-wheeler, I was finally able to breathe. They'd given up the chase. *Pansy ass...*

"Shit..." I swayed on my feet and my savior was there again to catch me.

CHAPTER

Wire

"Hey, hey, hold on!" She grabbed for me, holding on to my kutte for leverage, but her small frame was no match for mine. If I didn't get myself together I was going to fall right on top of her. I put my hand out to the wall, the sturdiness of it enough to keep me on my feet.

"Jesus Christ." She pulled my shirt up, it was soaked with blood and my life liquid was still pooling down by my boots. "We have to stop this bleeding."

She left me there, running to the kitchen to gather a few towels. She raced back over to me and pressed down *hard* with the towels.

"Son of a bitch!" I roared, banging the wall with my fist as the pain shot through my abdomen. She jumped back slightly at my outburst but never moved the towels. Max barked a few times, agitated that his owner was stuck with a screaming man.

"We have to get the blade out." I almost didn't recognize my voice, it was gravely and hoarse. Just getting those words out took all the breath I had.

"What?" She looked at me like I was crazy.

I pulled her hands away from my wound and plucked the metal jutting out from my side one time for good measure. Those bastards had snuck up on me while I was attending to my bitch. You never mess with a man who is working on his bike, its cowardly. Monte had buried the knife in my side and during the struggle, and the handle had broken off. It was in so deep that only the very edge was visible and was covered by muscle and tissue and blood.

The blood drained from her face. "No way, I have to get you to the hospital."

"No... hospitals," I slurred to her. "Jusss... Pull."

"I'm not prepared for this, hell I'm not even trained for this. What if you die or something?" She asked frantically, pressing the towels back to the wound, although a little softer now.

"Call my club." It was all I could say.

"What? What club?" She stared up at me, panic still in her eyes.

I raised my hand and slapped the patch on my heart, Wings of Diablo stitched into the supple leather.

"You have got to be kidding me!" She screeched.

The world spun upwards again and this time I couldn't stop myself from going down.

"Hey, Hey! Listen to me. Stay with me, ok. Just stay with me." The woman, with her shimmering gold eyes, was looking down at me. I was ok with this being the last thing I saw. "I'm going to get you help." Her trembling hand smoothed down my face, the soft texture strange against the roughness of my scruff. She bit her lip in worry, the creases more defined between her eyebrows. She didn't know me but she was worried.

I laid back and looked at the pink colored walls; at least I thought they were pink. It was too dark to tell. A cookie jar on the tiny kitchen island, an owl with wide eyes, a sign at the bottom asking *WHOOO stole the cookies?* The floor even smelled of Pine-sol, well the metallic smell of my blood was drifting in as well but I had to smile at the situation anyway.

How on earth did I end up here? My eyes finally drifted closed with that final question on my mind.

CHAPTER 3

Wire

A few days before...

"What the fuck do you mean your intel was wrong?"

Gin backed up against the wall. "Prez, I was told it was him. My guy has never steered me wrong before. I didn't even think to question his word."

WHOMP

Blood splattered the floor and the walls behind Gin as he covered his mouth. Prez had just punched him square in his jaw.

"I don't keep you here so that you can get your fucking information from half-ass druggies! I expect you to follow through on your orders and the order I gave was simple." Prez grabbed Gin by the back of the neck. He grimaced at the pressure, blood still dripping out of his mouth. "And what was the order I gave?"

Gin didn't say a word.

Prez pulled out his silver Beretta and pressed it squarely to Gin's jaw, right on the spot turning red from his previous assault. "Boy, don't make me blow your fucking face off!" Spit landed on Gin's face but he didn't even flinch. "What the fuck did I order you to do?" Prez screamed out.

"You told me to find out who fucked with our drop."

Prez smiled and rubbed the barrel of his gun against Gin's bald head as if he was combing hairs that weren't there. "Yes, exactly. Now tell me, what did you do?"

"Prez, I thought I…"

WHOMP

Another shot clear across his jaw. "No, you dickwad, you half-assed your duties and got your information from someone who was looking for his next score. How fucking dumb can you be? Of course, he was going to give you a name, and then on top of that, you didn't even check out the information. I swear on everything, I should end you right now." Prez stormed away, leaving Gin slumped against the wall.

Gin used to be the Ace in this club. He was on point all the time. He was our intel officer and had been for years, never once a screwup. Then about three months ago, for the first time, he couldn't deliver the intel that we needed, but no one thought anything about it. I mean, not everything is easily discoverable. But it didn't stop there, next it was half-truths, then intel that was nowhere near the caliber we needed to make conclusive decisions, and now this latest bombshell. His intel was just wrong.

We had a huge drop a week back, thirty-five bricks of pure white, one of the biggest loads we ever had. Normally we didn't deal in drugs; however, this offer was too good to turn down. We had planned it out for weeks. We knew who would be there and the role everyone would play. We met up with the Tears of Chaos in the exact spot we had agreed upon, and the money was about to exchange hands when one lone shot rang out. All hell followed.

Bodies flew all over the place, jumping behind cars and garbage containers.

"What the hell! Who started shooting?" Prez had screamed from behind a car.

"I don't know!" I had called back at him. Either way, neither side was going to back down now.

Bullets had rung through the air, whizzing past my ears and everything began to hum. It always happened when the guns started to pop off around me. The chaos almost lulled me. I pulled out my piece and let two rounds fly. I hit someone, not that it mattered to me. I heard

Rex scream. He was sprawled out in front of me, about ten feet to my right. He was dead before his body had a chance to settle on the concrete. Instead of being furious or sad or even vengeful, all I could think was, *"Ah, well, that's too bad."* I had known Rex since I was eight years old. We saw up our first skirt together, crawling under the pews in church.

The entire scenario had seemed to be happening to someone else, the norm for me. If there were one trait that anyone could use to describe me, it would be cold.

"Wire!" Clean called out to me, "Wire!"

I turned my head to him. "Yeah, what's up, man?" I asked as calm as ever like we were taking a fucking stroll through the park.

"Jesus Christ, bro. How are we going to get out of this shit?" A bullet pinged off the car that was hiding him, causing him to duck a little further. I didn't even flinch. I lifted my head, shot off a few more rounds and two more bodies dropped.

"Wire, bring your ass!" Prez was screaming from a truck. Where he was able to get the ride, I had no idea. Everyone jumped on the truck; on the sides, on the seats, on the hood, wherever they could find a spot, holding on as the truck burned rubber until we were out of dodge.

We had lost brothers from both clubs, and Gin had only one job. Find out who started the mess.

He came back with the name Scotty. Then we'd done what we do best, we rolled up and snatched little Scotty out of his bed and dropped into the club's pain chamber, with the club's creative pain dealer, me. You'd be surprised at how many people squeal like pigs, within just a few minutes of one on one time with me.

Scotty lasted about thirty seconds, swearing on everything that he didn't do it, that he had nothing to do with the deal going bad. Still, I had a job to do, and that was to make sure that he was telling me the absolute truth.

The fear in his eyes and the snot streaming down his face should've been enough but I needed to be sure.

They call me Wire because out of all the tools I could use and am one hundred percent proficient with, my very favorite is barbed wire;

9

the different lengths of the barbs, the edges either sharp or dull. Attached to a cricket board, on the edge of a steal poker, or used as a whip, the possibilities are endless.

"Please, please, I didn't do it. I'm only a prospect. I'll tell you whatever you want to know but I didn't do it." Blood poured down his arms, where the wires were still entwined with the sinews of his biceps.

I wrapped another length of wire around his upper thigh and pulled the metal with one hand then the other. The blades were dull on this one; still they were sharp enough to cut through his skin. They weren't clean cuts either, the skin and muscles were ripped away from his body little by little. He screamed, my mind completely blocking out the sound, only the words making it through.

"I didn't do it. I didn't do it," he sobbed, teeth chattering from shock and pain.

It had been over twenty minutes and he was missing a tricep, I had sliced that clean off. He would never run again, not with all the damage I had done to both his legs. The final straw, I had taken a three-inch barb and tore him from the base of his dick through his sack, straight through his taint slowly. He seized, he threw up, he called for god, he spoke in tongues, he fainted and then once again he said, "Please, I didn't do it."

I didn't know of anyone who had lived through that and would still lie. There was no way.

"Prez." I walked out of my chambers and up to him slowly. "Something is off here. I think we got the wrong guy."

"Impossible." He looked at me like I was spouting shit out of my mouth. "Gin says that is the guy. Maybe you are just losing your touch." He raised his eyebrows.

"Yeah?" I pointed to the door of my chamber and he followed. His eyes nearly bugged out of his head when he caught a glimpse of the boy. "You think you can do better?"

Prez ran out of the room and emptied the contents of his stomach on the floor of the club. "What the fuck! What did you do to him?"

"You asking me questions about my work now?" I didn't like anyone challenging or questioning me, the only thing stopping me from coming out my face to him was the fact that he was my president.

"Nah, you're right. There's no way the kid is lying." He shook his head, probably trying to get the image of Scotty out of his head. "Can he be patched up?"

"Patched up? Sure. He will never be the same again, though. I'm pretty sure I made him a eunuch, but sure I'll get the doc in here."

"You do that. I'm going to have a word with Gin." Prez stalked off, and I walked back into my chambers.

Poor Scotty.

CHAPTER 4

Wire

Prez was not one for killing folks that didn't need killing, so we patched little Scotty up the best that we could and sent him on his way. Straight back to the Tears of Chaos MC club, where he was a prospect. We knew that there was going to be some backlash, hell we knew there was going to be all out war, I just wasn't prepared to be caught out there alone. Unfortunately, that was exactly what happened, and here I was on this woman's linoleum floor, seeping from a hole in my side.

"What the fuck!" A deep voice called out.

"He said not to take him to the hospital. I swear to god he better no die on my floor!" A high pitched squeal this time.

"Did you pull this out?"

"Yeah, he told me to."

"Anything come out with it?"

"No!" Another high pitched squeal.

"I got to get him to the Doc. Fuck…"

I drifted off again, the sounds of those above me fading in and out.

"Didn't you hear me! I tried to! He said that he didn't want to go to the hospital!"

"Not a hospital, sweetness. We have a Doc at the club."

Bright lights burst behind my eyelids, jarring my semi-conscious state.

"What the Fuck! Get off of me." My eyes settled on the person standing above me. Clean was now trying to raise me off the floor.

"Listen, you bastard. You want to bleed out on this woman's floor?"

I looked down at the blood that was pooling beneath me. Clean was right. I had to get out of here right away, or I wasn't going to make it.

"Alright, alright... Let's go..." I slurred as I tried to roll over onto my knees, I didn't make it.

"Listen, I am going to pick you up and it's going to hurt like a bitch." Clean stared into my eyes, letting me know that he was serious. This was going to be fucking painful.

"On three..." Clean put his hands under my arms. "One...two..." Before he got to three, he wrenched me up.

I screamed as blood shot out from the hole in my side.

"Gut up, Wire!" Clean got me up to my feet with one arm draped around his shoulder. He was holding pressure on the wound as we began to walk out of the woman's house.

"Hey, sweetness..."

"Don't call me sweetness again, you barbarian! My name is Keeley!" She stood off to the side, eyes wide and nostrils flaring.

"Whatever, Keeley," Clean said her name with as much emphasis as possible, "you need to come with me."

"Are you crazy?"

"Nah, man leave her here," I said quietly. I wasn't sure either one of them heard me.

"Look, I have to drive the car. I can't hold him and apply pressure to the wound. If you don't want him to die, get your stuck-up ass in the car!" Clean screamed at her. If I had the energy, I would've punched him right in the gut. He was such a jackass.

"Fine!" She screamed back at him, not putting up any more of a fight.

"Oh shit. I think he's passing out..." That high voice screeched in my ear as the darkness began to cloud my vision.

"Just keep pressure on it!" Clean was screaming.

"What the fuck do you think I am doing, twiddling my goddamn thumbs?" Keeley yelled right back at him.

"Is everything an argument with you! Damn, woman!"

The car that we were in took a sharp left, making the wound on my side feel like it was ripping open. I groaned, causing them both to stop screaming at each other.

"Oh, you're awake! Thank God!" The woman looked at me with obvious concern. I guess things were going worse than I thought they were going.

"Motherfucker, you're messing up my ride. You better not die so you can get this shit cleaned out!"

"I am working on it, bro." I closed my eyes for a second, trying to get myself together. "Tell me we're getting close."

"Yeah, the compound is just there. Hold on."

I felt every bump in the road, the usual short road to my clubhouse seemed to take forever.

"We're here, bro."

"What do you want me to do?" Keeley asked, still hovering over me. It wasn't until I looked down that I saw that her hands were wrapped in a cloth and still holding down against the wound.

"Shit, you're going to have to come inside with me. I can't hold him on my own," Clean mumbled to her.,

Bringing her into the clubhouse was a bad idea. I knew it and from the way that he spoke to her he knew it too. We never let outsiders into our club; it was a rule. We never wanted to risk someone else being too familiar with our layout. It would be easy for someone to roll on up on us and take everyone out.

"Just keep your mouth shut and don't wander!" Clean said as we all kept moving forward. "I just need to get someone's attention."

The intense bass of the music made the covered windows rattle. The thick mist of perfume floating off the working girls smacked me dead in the face. I never knew why the bike bunnies always laid the perfume on so thick; it was nauseating. I opened my eyes slightly to see Clean and Keeley trying to talk to each other.

"Just drop me at my room, I'll be alright!" I screamed.

"Shut the fuck up."

"I thought there was a doctor here!" I heard Keeley belt out over the blaring music.

WIRE: A WINGS OF DIABLO MC NOVEL

"Oh shit! What the fuck happened to him?"

Gin ran up on me and pushed Keeley out of the way.

"Hey, shitstain. Where are your manners?" Keeley yelled behind us.

"Get her!" I yelled as hard as I could. It wasn't loud enough and Clean kept on walking with Gin now on my side instead of Keeley.

"Clean!" I straightened my legs, putting all the strength I had into stopping them moving. There was no way that we could leave her to wander the club, especially while there was a party going on. One of the other brothers might think that she was a bike bunny and take her.

Yet another rule, the biker bunnies were club property. No one asked them if they wanted to get fucked. They just pushed them against the wall and fucked them.

"What?" Clean looked at me. I guess I got his attention.

"Keeley." My mouth barely formed the word before he was looking all around us.

"Shit, where is the girl?" Clean yelled out over my head to Gin.

"What?"

"The chick we came in with? Where is she?"

"Oh, the Bunny? I left her back there." Gin started to move forward again.

"Fuck!" Clean roared. "She isn't a bunny!"

I felt my left side drop down as Clean went back to look for Keeley. He didn't come back.

"What the hell is this?" Prez walked up on Gin and me, jumping under my left arm and dragging me toward the back room.

"What happened to you, Wire?"

"Monte, he caught me alone. Had to hole up in some woman's house," I said through gritted teeth.

"Damn it. I knew this was going to blow back in our faces."

"Yeah, tell me about it."

"Get Doc upstairs right now!" Prez shouted to someone. "And shut this shit down; we got business to handle!"

Within seconds the music was off and the lights were back on. All the strippers and bike bunnies scurried around, trying to get out of the way. When the Prez called business, everything else stopped.

"I'm good, Prez, I can-" He cut me off before I could even complete my statement.

"Nah kid, go get this taken care of. You're leaking all over the floor." He lightly chuckled as he passed me over to one of the prospects to take me upstairs.

CHAPTER

Wire

I woke up the next morning, an IV in my arm and my side bandaged up. I felt beat up, but I was alive. That was more than I thought I was going to be. I had been beaten before but being that close to death was new for me. I was upset that I wasn't more emotional about it. Then again, I was never emotional about anything.

That was just how I was, since I was a little boy and my father's boot became the only way he knew how to discipline me, begging, fear, even real pain had flown out of my repertoire of emotional responses.

I jumped out of bed as quickly as I could. The pull of what I could only guess was stitching caused me to slow just a little.

"Yo, Clean, you down there?" I called out. If he were in the club, he would have heard me. The way our club had been designed meant the bottom level was an open floor, the second floor was all bedrooms, and the doors all led out to an indoor balcony style walkway. Many a brother had been pushed over the railing when they had had one too many to drink.

I always loved coming here, coming home. That rustic smell of the wood and whiskey always put me at ease.

"Yeah bro, I'm down here. You good?" Clean called to me from somewhere downstairs.

"Tell me you got some grub down there."

"Umm…" I heard the faint sound of rustling. "No, nothing." The bastard was hiding his food.

"I can hear you, dickwad."

"It's all done! There's no more!"

That means I had about thirty seconds to get downstairs before he shoved whatever he had in his mouth. I hobbled my ass to the door, looking off the balcony area. I could see that Clean was rummaging in the kitchen. Several others were laughing as they looked on from the sidelines. I rushed down the stairs the best I could. My mouth was watering; I was so hungry. Yesterday's ordeal must have drained me.

"Stop being a bastard," I said as I stopped behind him.

He sucked his teeth and turned around. A whole half of a hoagie still on a plate in front of him.

"You weren't going to share?"

"I'm going to go with a strong no, on that one," Clean said while handing me the untouched half of sandwich that was on his plate.

"You two finished kissing up on each other, or should I give you a few more seconds?" Prez called out from behind us. He was standing in front of church as a few of the key members filed out behind him. They must have just finished a meeting.

Clean and I put our game faces on and walked towards Prez; something must have been going down.

"Prez, what's up?" I asked.

"Well, there's no real good way to put this." Prez shook his head. "We need to go make peace with Chaos."

"What the fuck?" Clean puffed out his chest. Out of all the crews in the area, Chaos was like our arch enemies. We've never gotten along with them. We always stayed on opposite ends of the county, making sure to stay out of each other's way. Now Prez was telling us that we needed to tuck tail and ask for forgiveness? I was with Clean on this one. I didn't even remotely think that my pride would let me do something like that.

"Prez, that's just going to show weakness."

"Kid, we fucked up. What we did to that Scotty boy was more than just a beatdown, we destroyed that kid's life. Chaos is going to keep coming at us until we make it right. I am down just like anyone else in this club to lay my life for my kutte but not over a dumbass' mistake. You gotta learn to pick the right battles."

I knew what he was saying was right. We had to make amends, but knowing it was the right thing to do still didn't make the idea any easier to swallow.

"Ok, Prez, when do we move out?" I asked, squaring up, ready to take my licks even if they were coming from Monte and his crew.

"You must be out of your mind to call us up here if you think it's going to be anything less than death for you and yours," Monte called out from his line.

It was a good old fashion stare down. We were out in the fucking middle of no-mans-land, decaying buildings on either side of us, no witnesses, guns cocked and loaded at everyone's side.

"Monte, I called you out here to talk like men. I'm man enough to know that retribution has to be paid when my crew fucks up." Prez called out, the spearhead of our line.

"When your crew fucks up?" Monte chuckled lightly, "You think what you had done to Scotty was just a mere fuck up? It was an unprovoked attack! You brought war on yourself and now you think a couple of words are going to fix it. Nah, not happening!" Monte yelled. There were about two car lengths between the Wings of Diablo and the Tears of Chaos. The club members lined up side by side with the Prez out in front. The air was crackling with tension, the muscle in my trigger finger tense with the need to pull. It would only take one second, one motion to lay Monte out, and after he tried to gut me on the side of the road, I was more than willing to lay him out.

"Monte, are you going to hear us out or are you just going to talk shit?" Prez yelled back.

"I'm trying not to hear the shit you're sayin', but if y'all want to sweep this under the rug, you can send me over that fucker, Wire."

The air around me stilled, they wanted me dead in a ditch somewhere. Prez had two choices here. He could give me up to them and let this drop and everyone would be safe for now or he could tell them all to kick rocks and die and we'd have a shoot out right here.

"You expect me to believe that if I just hand over Wire to you, that'll be the end of it? I have some serious doubts."

"It doesn't matter what you think; I'm telling you what I want. Are you going to give it to me or not?"

I dropped my head and took a deep breath; I would be fine if he decided to send me on my way, I wouldn't feel any differently about my crew if they thought that I was expendable.

"Well, you know what? I just don't think that is going to happen today."

"Today, tomorrow or next week. No matter to me, I will have," Monte pointed the barrel of his black Smith and Wesson at me, "his head on a platter."

"You can try to get him if you want," Prez spat back at him as he began to back away. I looked up at my Prez with just a little more respect. He had chosen the hard road and I was grateful.

We turned with our Prez as he went towards his truck. This meeting was over and so far, nothing crazy had popped off. Yet.

"You think you can just turn your back on me?" Monte screamed while we all strode off. I did agree with him on one thing though, turning our backs on them was a bad idea.

Things were silent as we made our way back toward our bikes and cars.

Click-click, click-click, click-click

The sound was barely audible, but it was getting closer and closer. I turned to see a pitbull almost on Prez's ass.

"Oh shit, Prez, watch out!' I yelled as I pulled my Glock out, shooting twice at the dog right before he got to Prez.

The bullets began to fly then. All of Chaos and Diablo dived for whatever cover they could find and opened fire.

I ducked to the side behind a building. This worn-down area was full of abandoned houses; the windows and walls were all the protection I needed at the moment. I sank down and let the whizz of the bullets flying by my ears lull me into a trance. A soft hum descended on my muscles, and I was at ease amongst the chaos.

"Wire!" *Was someone screaming for me?*

"Wire! Get your ass away from there, that awning is going to collapse any second!"

I looked up above my head, the drywall that was attached to the awning was raining down white specs of debris with every bullet that hit it.

"Wire." A voice screamed for me again.

I stood up slowly, not even thinking about the bullets that were flying past me. I lifted my cannon, aimed at the closest person to me and fired. The bullet hit square between his eyes. I watched as his now lifeless body dropped to the floor. His head made a sickening sound like a bat hitting a ball out of the park. *I wonder if there's a game on, weren't the Yanks supposed to play today?*

I strolled over to where the rest of my crew was and waited for the next order. The sound of Prez roaring snapped me back to the present.

"No!" Prez shouted, trying to come out of cover. Everyone near him was holding him back, trying to pull him away from where he was trying to reach. I looked over the barrier that I had knelt in front of and saw that Max, our club VP, was lying face down on the ground. He wasn't moving. If both he and Prez were to get shot today, our club would be in fucking disarray. They were right to keep him from trying to run out into the open.

"Come on. We have to get out of here as soon as we can." Clean smacked me on the shoulder, as he loaded another clip into his gun.

I turned my head as I heard the telltale sign of more trouble on the way... Cops.

"We gotta go now!" The bullets stopped flying as everyone on both sides began to scramble to vehicles and bikes and get out of dodge. The last thing anyone wanted to do was to get pinched. *Jail isn't for everyone.*

We jumped on our bikes and into our cars, speeding away from the scene, leaving the bodies of our VP and three other brothers lying there in their own blood. Prez came here today to see if there could be some degree of peace. Peace was definitely out of the question now.

CHAPTER 6

Wire

The club was in mourning. It had been so long since we lost someone from the table, the higher-ups in the club. Losing Max was going to cause a lot of problems for the club, and replacing him would cause even more. Max was the level headed one. He usually kept Prez chomping at the bit when it came to war with other clubs, and now there was no one to hold him back. I saw a lot of fights in our future.

Tonight though, the only thing on the club's mind was Max. Most people when they mourn, cry, fight or hole up somewhere. Not the Wings of Diablo, no, we party and we party hard. The entire complex was bumping with rock music, booze and club bunnies. The bunnies lived for days like this. I wouldn't be surprised if nine months from now, there were a few babies.

This was one of the main problems with the bunnies. They wanted to be ol' ladies so bad that they would do anything, even get pregnant on purpose to be a part of the crew. Prez had a solution for that and so far, it seemed to be working. The girls were now responsible for the condoms; if the crew were too drunk, the condom broke, or had a hole in it, there was hell to pay. Though no one knew what kind of hell, since they'd never tried to find out. The threat was real and it was working, there had been no babies in the past two years within the crew.

I scanned the crowd in front of me, the skinny stripper on stage no longer keeping my attention. She wasn't my type; no thighs, no ass, no meat at all. It was a surprise that she was able to remain standing straight with the size of her fake tits. I was more concerned that one of her tricks would send her flying from the pole, but none did. I was bored.

I saw one girl with bright blue hair, and as startling as that was it fit her. It was short and had a curl to it. She turned to look at me and started dancing. Her outfit was what concerned me, she had on the customary thong and her tits were out. She had the typical body of a stripper, nothing to write home about. What caught my attention though, was the one piece of clothing she chose to wear. Lace sleeves connected around her neck with a jeweled sort of contraption, they flowed all the way to her fingertips covering nothing but her arms. Why would she go through so much trouble to cover her arms? There was only one possible reason; she was a fucking druggie. I turned around immediately. I was amazed she was even let in here. We may transport from time to time, but anyone caught using drugs in or around our compound was beat to shit then left out on the curb. I wasn't about to get my dick sucked by a drug fiend. You never knew what kind of shit they had in their system.

I turned to the other side and scanned the room. Cherry was free, she was a usual here in the club, and was a legit dancer and ballerina before she came to us. She could do some flexible things in the bed. Many of us liked Cherry.

Today she had on booty short panties and a bra of some type, except the bra had no fabric. It was just the straps and the hard wire part that goes under the boobs. *What use was that?*

I didn't understand the outfit, but it was sexy as hell for some reason. Her tits seemed to sit right up, her ass looked plump, and her stomach was toned. Yeah, Cherry would do tonight. I kept her eye contact as I walked over to a chair. I sat down and beckoned her over. She walked towards me with purpose. The smile on her face was unmistakable. I was a favorite among the club bunnies. I'd asked one of them one day. It wasn't like I actively tried to make them feel good, hell I barely said three words to any of them. All I wanted to do was get my dick wet, drop my load and take a fucking nap, but according to them my dick was big enough that I didn't need to put in any work, I filled their honey holes up and it was easy for them to come no matter what I did. *Good for them, I guess.*

When she got to where I was sitting, she straddled my lap, pushing her small tits in my face, she barely had a handful, but they were sitting up proud in that outfit she had on.

She started to dance, but she must've doused herself in perfume, the smell was making me sick.

"Turn around."

She did so without question, she bent over and began to grind her ass on me. I was thoroughly mesmerized by her, and she knew what she was doing. I ran my hand up her spine and she jumped like she wasn't expecting me to touch her. She looked over her shoulder and gave me a coy smile. I watched her eyes as she went back to dancing on me, instead of looking at her own body or even closing her eyes she was completely focused on Larry, one of my brothers. She was watching him while she was working my dick. I didn't like that shit at all.

"Get the fuck off of me." I pushed her off my lap, she barely had enough warning to put her hands out to catch herself. "If you want Larry, go over there and get him. Don't waste my time."

"No no, that's not it at all, Wire! I was looking at the new girl, making sure she was keeping up."

I know bullshit when I hear it and this was bullshit at its finest. Everyone knew that Cherry had a thing for Larry, but we never mixed business with pleasure. It would be an impossible road to go from bunny to ol' lady. Hell, no one had ever tried.

"Let's get out of here. I already know what you like anyway." She rubbed her hand down my stomach and pressed her palm heavily onto my contained manhood. She massaged me for a second before grabbing my hand and leading me towards my room. She was right; I just wanted to fuck, the lap dance wasn't necessary.

I was less than impressed after her show outside, but I would forget about it. I mean, the only people that were off-limits here were the women that were claimed, she wasn't. So that made her fair game.

"Wire, you here with me?"

"Don't talk. Get on your knees." Maybe I wasn't fully there with her, I was still thinking about the events of the day, but she wasn't going to become my shoulder to lean on suddenly.

24

"You got it..."

I covered her mouth with my hand, roughly. "One more time, do... not... talk." I let go when she just smiled up at me. I knew she had gotten the hint.

She took her time, pulling off my pants and underwear as she used her nails to scratch along my skin. I guess my body was game for whatever Cherry had planned. I was at full attention, like a rod of steel just swaying in the wind. The passion and need that I once felt as a teenager when it came to sex had long since ebbed, and now it was purely for relaxation. After a good orgasm, I slept like a baby. No nightmares.

I let my body fall back on the bed as her warm mouth took me in. She was able to take more of me than most of the bunnies could. She was practically the only person that I let suck me off. My philosophy with the bunnies was if you aren't good at it, why do you even attempt it. Nothing pissed me off more than a girl that had to gag every ten seconds.

I let her stay on her knees for a while. I was nice and loose when I pulled her up by her hair.

"Strip."

She was out of her panties and bra and climbing up my body before I could blink. I had to smile at her obvious enthusiasm. She wrapped her arms around my neck, pressing her breasts against my chest. Even on her tiptoes, she was still at least a whole head shorter than me, so with both of us lying down, we seemed to be on an even field. She curled her fingers at the base of my neck, playing with the hairs there. She bit her lip slightly and raised herself toward my mouth.

"I don't know what you're thinking, but if you try to kiss me, I'm tossing you the hell out." I looked her straight in the eye. Every one of the bunnies knew I didn't like to be kissed. It held no attraction for me and just felt like spit and mucus moving around in my mouth.

She just looked at me through her eyelashes and shook her head. She knew better. She cocked her head to the side and kissed me lightly on the neck.

What the hell is she playing at?

I grabbed her wrist and rolled over on top of her, pressing down on her back so that her head and chest were flat against the bed, her ass sticking up in the air waiting for me. I reached over to the side table and retrieved a condom. There was no way I was going raw with this girl.

Within a few seconds, I was set. I rubbed the head against her sex to make sure she was nice and wet.

"Mmm… Wire." She wiggled her butt and pressed back against me.

"I hope you're ready for me." I could feel her entrance was soaking wet, but I also knew that many a girl had tapped out before I could even bury myself to the hilt once.

"I'm ready, so ready." She wiggled a bit more.

I steadied myself at her entrance and with one swift movement, pushed myself as far as I could get, which was only about halfway. She tightened up, stopping my motion.

"Cherry," I growled out, ready to pull out and kick her out of the room. I had no time for a half-assed fuck today. I was tired and wanted to get some decent sleep.

"No… sss ok, ok," she mumbled against the pillow, and I felt her push back. I pushed the rest of the way in and let the warmth overtake me. I pulled out once and she cried out. The tempo I picked up was ruthless. I wanted this over as soon as possible.

"Oh… Oh… My god, Wire, Jesus." She was moaning and carrying on, not surprisingly. It wasn't the typical high pitched squealing that I usually heard coming from other rooms, this was deep and guttural. She clawed at the sheets, trying to get a grip. I wrapped my hand in her hair, pulling her head up from the bed and letting her midsection bow downward. She yelped at the sudden change of position. I leaned back a bit. I wanted to hit everything inside her.

"Oh please, oh please," Cherry cried out as her legs and midsection began to contract and shake, vibrate even. I thought she was going to tell me to stop. "Don't stop, Wire. I am so close, so close." She grabbed the hand gripping her shoulder and bit down on my thumb, hard enough to cause me to hiss out in pain. I pulled my hand away and swatted her hard on her plump ass.

"Oh, oh… oh….."

I kept my pace, while Cherry tensed, seeming to stop breathing altogether. Then her body jerked a couple of times, and she let out a whoosh of air as she flopped back on the bed, completely spent but still mewling as I continued to pound into her with a drive one could call well motivated.

"Wirrrrre!" She screamed my name again as I upped the pace, harder and deeper. I needed it hard and deep all the time. I could finally feel my balls starting to tingle. It was my turn.

I clenched my jaw and felt each pulse as it shot out of me and into the condom. I was at ease almost instantly. All of my muscles relaxed except for my dick; it was still hard as a rock. It was rare that I could fuck enough for it to go down.

I pulled out of Cherry, not even caring that she was still grinding herself down on me. I'd had what I wanted and from the way she'd been screaming so did she, at least once.

"Get out."

Cherry looked over her shoulder, giving me a small frown. Her makeup was all messed up, her hair was all over the place and she had managed to lose an earring somewhere on my bed.

"Ah, Wire, I don't think that you mean that." She turned towards me, her eyes glued to my still massive, hard member. "I can go another round, no problem."

"I said get the fuck out, you're done." I grabbed a pair of basketball shorts from the dresser, looking over my shoulder only once. Another reason Cherry was a favorite; she knew not to press. She was already fixing herself and heading out the door.

I closed the door behind her as she left, hoping to drown out the bone rattling bass from the party still going full blast downstairs. I closed my blinds and locked my door. I'd take a quick shower to get the stink of Cherry off me and then knock out time. I couldn't even wait.

"Wire!"

What the fuck? Why am I dreaming about a man?

The loud ass bang on my door let me know that I was not dreaming of a man, but rather someone was at my door banging like a crazy person.

"Wire, I know you're in there. Wake the hell up. You got a problem." Clean banged again on my door.

"GO...AWAY!" I pulled the cover over my head. I love my sleep. I don't get much of it, so when I do, no one had better wake me up unless they were dying or suicidal. Unfortunately, Clean just liked to press on that button from time to time to see if I would indeed beat his ass. I always did.

"Brother, I can't. They got Keeley cornered in here. What do you want to do," he shouted through my still closed door.

Keeley!

The chick from the other night? She was in my club? How? Why? The questions just kept coming. This was bad in so many ways for her. Nothing was stopping the other members from just taking what they wanted from her.

I hopped out of bed quicker than I would've thought possible, but I was fully clothed and out of my bedroom before Clean had the chance to knock on the door again.

"What the hell is she doing here?"

"Hell, how should I know? I saw Gin, Archer, and Larry around her in the corner, but I'm sure she'll draw a bigger crowd," he said as we made our way down the stairs. The party was still going full force, but a lot of the regulars were already in their rooms. I could hear the high pitched porno wails coming through the doors.

"Where is she?" I asked Clean again. He was swaying a bit but I could see that he was trying to get his mind right to help me.

"She was just over there a minute ago."

I rushed off in the direction that he pointed. That woman saved my life when she didn't have to, the least I could do was to make sure no one fucked with her in my club, although she deserved what she got for just showing up here. I turned the corner, and right near the bar, I could hear her, even over the loud music.

"You can get your damn hands off me. I asked a question. Do you know where Dillon is?" The attitude was oozing off every word.

WIRE: A WINGS OF DIABLO MC NOVEL

My dick was hard again at the sound of my name coming off her tongue. Dillon was my civilian name. I hadn't heard anyone use it in years. I liked how it sounded coming from her lips. I liked it a lot.

"Nah, sweetness, we don't got no Dillon here," Gin yelled over the music, "but I can show you a good time."

"Yea, then I'm next," Larry said.

"I just want to watch someone take that ass," Archer said lastly, laughing.

I growled low in my chest. I had this incredible need to protect her even though I barely knew her.

"Sorry, boys. I'm not here for that kind of good time. I just wanted to talk to Dillon for a minute."

"Sorry Princess, you walk in those doors, and that's exactly the kind of good time you're looking for. Now I don't want this to hurt unless that's how you like it?" Gin said again.

"Leave me alone!" She was screaming now.

"If you don't back away from her, we're going to have a problem."

CHAPTER 7

Wire

"No dice, brother. She isn't patched up, so she's fair game. I saw her first." Gin stood with his back to Keeley, the fear still plastered on her face as she looked to me for help.

"I don't give a shit if she isn't patched up. I am telling you right now that she is off-limits."

"And I'm telling you that she is not." Gin stepped up closer to me. He was staring me down, waiting for his chance. Gin and I never really were the best of friends, but there was always a tiny bit of respect for each other. The minute he touched her, the respect was gone.

"You think so? You want me to prove how off-limits she is?" I clenched my fists and stepped up a little bit closer to him.

"Come on, Gin. It's not worth all this." Archer grabbed Gin's arm, trying to pull him away.

"Fuck that, golden boy here don't get to just up and change the rules when he sees fit. She walked up into hell, and there's no way she leaves unscathed." Gin ripped his hand away from Archer.

"I say she does. If you've got a problem with that, you can fight me or get the fuck out my way." I waited, but Gin had no rebuttal. I reached behind him and pulled Keeley toward me, whipping her behind me before she could even think to protest.

"You willing to take on one of your brothers for this piece of ass? Who the hell-"

"I am going to tell you this one more fucking time! She is off limits! Now either throw your fucking hands or get the hell out of my face!" I roared at Gin. The surprise on his, Archer, and Larry's face was enough to let me know that they got the point. I was never angry. I never showed any emotion. I'd never had any reason to show any emotion, but this was different. Keeley, this woman, she wasn't tainted by my club or my life. She would not be harmed here; I wouldn't allow it. Gin smirked at me a bit, but just stood there staring at me.

Archer and Larry shook their heads, walking away to find some other tail to mess with. There were more than enough women to go around. Gin would be thinking about the next girl in just a few minutes.

I turned around, pulling Keeley away from the area.

"Fucking pussy," Gin mumbled under his breath, and even though the music was still pumping, I heard it clearly. It seemed like I was just waiting for the excuse to knock his teeth down his throat. Before Clean could catch my arm, I turned and swung full force at Gin, connecting with a sickening crack against his jaw. His eyes glazed over for a second before the veins in his head and neck began to strain through his skin. He threw himself at me, his hands resembling bear paw punching me in the sides. The taste of iron filtered into my mouth as I raised my knee to dislodge him. The hum descended on me and I could no longer feel any pain. I could see him throwing his hands and could feel the motion of my body as it accepted his blows, but there was no pain associated with it. There never was.

I swung my elbow down onto his face. I could feel his bone crunch underneath mine.

I wonder if I hit him again if he will die?

I ducked as he swung a wild haymaker at my face. He was too dazed this time to make contact. The sweat from his brow dripped down the side of his face and onto the collar of his kutte, making the one spot of worn leather darker than the rest. I fixated on that until my head snapped straight back as he clocked me straight in the nose. His big arm rose over his head as he steadied himself to deliver another blow. I backed away as he tried to swing again. I caught his arm, the small hairs on his forearm, giving my sweating palm some traction to pull him in and around. I wound my thick arms around his neck, squeezing enough for him to foam at the mouth. He was slapping at my arms, clawing and scratching.

31

"Wire!"

"Wire!" Someone else was screaming my name, but it sounded so far away. Whoever it was, I hoped they didn't need me. Right now, I had to deal with Gin. He was still moving.

"Dillon!" The force of that name smacked me in my face. I sucked in a deep breath and stared up at the person calling my birth name.

"Let go. You're going to kill him!" Keeley pleaded with me.

I looked down at Gin. I had thought he was still moving when, in fact, it was my brothers pulling at me that was moving his body. Gin was out cold, and I didn't know how long ago he'd stopped breathing. I dropped him immediately.

"What the shit, Wire?" Prez pushed me out of the way and went to tend to Gin. After a few tense seconds, Gin groaned. He was alive. I let out a deep breath. I didn't feel bad for beating his ass, and I would never willingly kill my brother. I was just not wired that way.

"He'll be ok," I mumbled under my breath. Prez heard it.

"I couldn't give two shits. I don't know what that was about, but you need to step off for a bit, Wire. I don't know what he's going to do when he wakes up, but I doubt he is going to be too happy."

"You're right, Prez. I'm going to go cool off." I turned, grabbed Keeley's hand, and started to walk away.

"Wait a minute."

I turned around to see Prez walking up behind me.

He nodded at Keeley. "Who's this lovely piece?"

I knew that look he was giving her, desire. I couldn't fight my Prez over Keeley no matter what she'd done for me.

"This is Keeley. She isn't a bunny. I don't know what she's doing here, but I plan to find out. She saved my life." I hoped that would be enough to appease him, enough to get him to not ask for her.

"She's what you fought Gin about?"

I nodded once.

A spark of recognition blazed in his eyes, and a half-smile curled up his lips. "Ok. Take her on out then, Wire."

I didn't know what to make of that look, but I was happy that he was giving me an out.

CHAPTER

8

Wire

I dragged Keeley out of the bar as fast I could, not caring she was tripping behind me or that she was telling me to let of her. All of this shit was because this woman just decided to stroll into my club looking for me, calling me by my real name.

Things weren't clicking in my head.

How the hell did she know my real name?

I grabbed her arm tighter than I had before, and once we made it to her truck, I slammed her against it.

"Ow! What the hell is your problem?" She yelled out.

"Right now, my problem is you!" I stared at her. She had clear gold eyes. I didn't even know eyes came in that color, but here was a set looking straight at me, clearly pissed off. "What the hell are you doing in my club? And how do you know my name?"

"Lucky for you, I can knock out both those questions with one answer." She went to reach inside her purse. I grabbed her wrist before she could make any contact with the bag. She raised an eyebrow at me. "Paranoid much?"

I was paranoid. I let her hand go, but I watched as she reached into her bag, a little annoyed when she couldn't find what she was looking for right away.

Damn women and their bags.

Finally, a small smirk played on her lips as she began to pull something out of the great abyss that was her purse.

It was black, thick, worn, leather.

Oh shit.

It was my wallet. Instinctively I patted my pockets and low and behold my wallet was missing.

"How did you even get this?" I snatched it from her hand and placed it back in my pocket, where I thought it'd been all along.

"You remember that day you were bleeding to death on my floor?" She said with a big fake ass smile.

I barely grunted in response.

"Well, it seems you may have left your wallet, and here I was trying to be the good samaritan and return it to you." She rolled her eyes and looked away. "Look at the thanks I get for that."

Now I felt like a grade-A asshole.

"Yeah, well thanks for that. I didn't even realize it was gone." I shrugged as I opened the passenger door for her.

"Why aren't I driving my car?"

"My club doesn't take no for an answer. I'm pretty sure one of them is going to try and follow you home," I said nonchalantly.

"What the freak?" She asked as she hopped in and looked over her shoulder.

They probably wouldn't follow her, but I still wanted to make sure that she made it home safe.

I climbed in the front seat, and we started on our way.

"This is crazy. Here I was thinking that I was going to drop off this stupid wallet, and not only do I get felt up, but now I have to worry about people stalking me. Geez, never again." She huffed out, crossing her arms.

"Well, if it makes you feel any better, I'm very grateful."

She turned her head to look at me and stared daggers at my head. "Nope, I don't feel any better about it at all."

I gave a slight chuckle.

"I'm amazed you remember where I lived. I figured you missed it when you were passed out."

"No, I am pretty good with things like that."

I watched her dig her keys out of her purse and open the front door to her house. Max was already at the door, waiting for her to walk in. She walked in and opened the door further so that I could come in. I wasn't expecting to do a house visit, but I wasn't about to turn her down. Max trotted right up to me, sniffed around a few times, barked once and went about his business. So much for a guard dog.

"He already knows you," Keeley answered before I could even ask her a question about Max.

"If you say so."

"It's the truth. If you were a stranger who walked in without me, he would have ripped off your face."

I had no choice but to roll my eyes at that. "Sure."

She shrugged and made her way into the living area. I tried to follow behind her, but she stopped me right in my tracks with a glare.

"Boots."

I looked down at my feet. My cruddy, old biker boots would need to come off. I toed them off and left them by the corner near the door before I followed her into the living room. Her space was simple but functional.

There was a TV though it looked as if it hadn't been turned on in ages. The couch was plush and big, a nice purplish color. She had throw pillows all over the place, many with girly sayings like "Pass me the wine" or "Girl Power". I had to turn one around before I would even sit down. It was a shot to my masculinity. There was a doggy bed for Max in the corner and stacks upon stacks of books in the other corner. Surprisingly they all looked like textbooks. I briefly wondered if she was still in school, but the curves on her body indicated there was no way. She was all woman.

"So, Keeley…"

"So Dillon…" she replied, mocking my tone.

Again, my dick twitched at the sound of my name on her lips. I knew if I wanted to get her in bed, I'd have to put in some work. The club had me spoiled. Usually, I'd just wait until I got with one of the bunnies.

"Seriously, thank you for bringing my wallet back. I would have never noticed it was gone until I needed it."

"Yeah, no problem…" She hesitated. "Well, the attempted groping by your buddies was a bit of a problem and... wait, did they follow me home?"

I laughed a bit at her change of pace. "I didn't see anyone, but I will check again when I leave."

"Crap! How are you going to get back? We used my car."

"It's fine. I'll take a cab. Why are you kicking me out already?"

She sucked her teeth and got off the couch, depositing one hand on her hip. "Oh, please. Don't be so stupid. You can stay as long as you like. You want a beer or something?" She stood in front of me, waiting for an answer.

"You don't even know me? Why would you invite me into your home?" I asked, honestly confused by this girl.

"Dillon, I've had..." She stopped speaking when she saw the big smile on my face.

"What? Why are you smiling like that?" She asked.

"It has been decades since anyone has called me my real name. People usually call me Wire."

"Wire?" She wrinkled her nose. "Why?"

"You don't want to know."

"Fine. Well, do you want me to stop calling you, Dillon?"

"Absolutely not."

She laughed lightly, then continued, "Like I was saying, I've had my hand basically touching your inner organs. If I can't trust you, then who the heck can I trust? Besides I have Max. One word from me and he will kill you."

I laughed out loud at that. The big fluff ball looked as harmless as any animal I'd ever seen. At the moment, he was curled up in the corner.

She raised one eyebrow at me, standing with crossed arms over her chest.

She pursed her lips and whispered, *"Prijetnja."*

The most menacing growl I'd ever heard echoed through the room. The once docile Max was now up and pacing towards me, his lips curled back, beady eyes trained on me. I went to move my arm, and he barked viciously. I knew that if I tried to get up or moved too suddenly, that dog would be at my throat. I stayed as still as I could manage. Even breathing seemed like it would tip my fate in the wrong direction.

"You've made your point," I whispered without moving my eyes from the dog.

"Have I now?" Keeley asked calmly.

"Yeah, call him off before I have to shoot him."

"Your arm would be off your body before you ever had a chance to reach for your gun."

I believed her.

Just to prove her point, Max barked again, inching forward slightly.

"Keeley!"

She spoke again in that strange tongue, "*Ljubiti.*"

Max straightened up and began to trot up to me.

"Keeley…" I was apprehensive. He was no longer growling and barking, but I had seen him change in a second before.

He stopped in front of me and jumped up, his front paws on my thighs.

I nearly screamed when he jumped up further and started to lick my face. I wanted to laugh in relief.

"Get your fucking dog."

"Max, get down."

He leapt down off my lap and trotted back towards his bed in the corner as if nothing had happened.

I got up, walking over to the kitchen to splash some water on my face in an attempt to clean his spit off of my face.

"You better be careful with him doing that to people. Someone is going to hurt him one day."

She laughed out loud. "Shall we have another demonstration?"

"No!" I shouted. I would be staying away from that dog for a long while.

"No worries. I can take care of myself." She walked away and went to sit back on the couch.

I plopped down on the opposite side. "Really, I have to doubt that. You wouldn't even know if you were in danger."

"You're so quick to judge when you know nothing about me. Especially when I know so much about you."

"Is that so? Well, enlighten me, princess."

"You have a gun in the small of your back, and one tucked in the side of your boot that's now on the other side of the room. You do a lot of work with your hands, probably with a weapon that leaves those long scars. I would say you are an enforcer, meaning that you probably wouldn't have the slightest problem killing someone. You're loyal to your club, you were holding back your punches today with that bald guy, and when you thought you'd choked him to death, you held your breath until he made a sound. I would say for anyone to get to you, they'd have to come from the inside." She blinked at me innocently.

She was right on every account. The gun in my back was usually invisible, especially under my shirt and kutte. *How did she know all this stuff?* None of it was in my wallet for damn sure.

"What, are you a cop?" I raised my eyebrow at her. I was hoping that she wasn't.

"No, sir. I am a scientist."

I had to laugh at that one. "Get the hell out of here."

"This is no laughing matter. It's the truth."

My jaw dropped. I had spent all my life with the druggies, miscreants and thugs. I'd never met anyone who was more than a stripper or store clerk in my life, and she was a scientist. I was awestruck.

"Well, I guess that's why you know so much. You're a freaking Einstein."

"You mean I'm a freaking John Muir?"

"Who?"

She shrugged. "I am an environmental scientist, less physics, more plants."

"Ah, I got you."

"You want a beer or something like that?"

"Yeah, I'll take a brew." I sat back and watched as she got off the couch to go back to the kitchen. "None of that explains how you would be able to determine I'm a fighter or that I have two guns in my possession."

She walked back and dropped a bottle of Corona in my hand.

"Let's just say it was more about guns and enforcers when I was growing up then it was about trees and rivers."

So, she grew up around this, another puzzle piece about the lovely Keeley.

I nodded at her as I took a swig. She stared out her window as she took a swig of her beer.

I was very comfortable here, too comfortable. That was my cue. It was time for me to go.

I took the rest of the beer and tossed it down my throat. "Well, I guess it's time to go." I stood up and walked over to my boots as she followed softly behind me.

"Ok, well, it was nice to see you not bleeding on my floor. You're much taller than I remember."

I turned around and noticed that she was at about nose height to me. She had to be about five foot nine or five foot ten. "So are you." I laughed slightly. I looked around her small kitchen, finding a pen and paper.

"Are you really going to waste a tree right now?" She rolled her eyes and took out the cell phone she had in her back pocket. "Just put whatever in here."

I took the phone from her and programmed my number into it. I smiled to myself when I deleted Wire and wrote Dillon instead. Yeah, she would be the only one to call me that, and I was just fine with that.

CHAPTER 9

Wire

"What the fuck are you smiling about?" Prez asked as I walked back into the club after the hour-long trek from Keeley's house.

"What are you talking about?" I fixed my face back into its customary scowl. I hadn't even realized that I was smiling until Prez brought it up.

"Yeah, whatever. So, who's the dame?"

"I already told you. When all that shit went down with Monte and the Tears, she saved my ass."

"Is that right? So, what the hell was she doing in the club today?"

"The crazy girl had my wallet. I didn't even know it was missing until she pulled it out."

"I was wondering with all that Dillon shit. I'm assuming she got it from your ID?"

"Yup."

"She seemed cool about it."

"Uh… yeah." I didn't know what direction Prez was going in, but I was going to play it safe.

"Too cool?"

"What do you mean, Prez?"

"She with another crew?"

That would be one of the biggest breaches of loyalty. You never bring another crew to your home without the Prez's consent; it just didn't happen.

"What the fuck? I would never-"

"Don't sit here and get defensive with me, boy."

My hackles were up for sure. I was pissed he'd even think that of me, but I couldn't show my emotions.

"I ain't getting defensive!"

"You are!" He shrieked back at me. "I am just saying pussy can change a man and the way she got your nose all open-"

I was done with this conversation. I turned and walked away from him. He didn't know what he was talking about, and I wasn't going to stand around and have him say all that shit when it wasn't true. My nose wasn't open. It wasn't.

I laid in my bed, still pissed off that Prez could have been so wrong about me. I mean, just because he had his ol' lady and would pretty much eat the shit directly out of her ass, didn't mean that I was going down that road. *Never.* Fuck, I'd never even been in a relationship before, and I'd never wanted to be in one. I didn't want the headache.

bzzzz, bzzzz

My phone buzzed. I picked it up, thinking it was Clean or one of my other brothers calling, only to see a number I didn't know.

"Speak," I barked into the receiver.

"Jeez, how abrasive."

Keeley.

I was pissed off the minute I felt my lips try to curl up in a smile.

"What do you want?"

"Ok... well, I just wanted to know if it was cool to go out. You said your club might follow me."

"Do you have fucking eyes?"

"Excuse me?"

"Well, I guess you don't have ears either or are you just a deaf twat?"

"Who the hell do you think you're talking to?" I could hear the steam coming out of Keeley's ears through the phone.

"Look, if you want to take a ride, just say so. My dick is free for the evening."

"Oh, fuck you, Dillon!"

"Anytime you want, Keeley."

She hung up on me, leaving me at the end of the phone, wondering why the hell I did that.

She'd been nothing but good to me and the minute Prez ruffled my feathers about her, I lashed out. What a dickwad move.

"Wire. Get your ass down here."

I hopped out of bed, trying hard to put the conversation with Keeley out of my head. I was having a hard time doing that.

I walked out in my typical outfit, dark washed jeans, black worn t-shirt, my biker boots and my kutte. I didn't need anything else. I didn't think I even had any other colors in my closet besides black and dark blue.

The dark blue shirt was by accident. I was so fucking drunk one day I couldn't tell the difference between the two colors and ended up buying the wrong color.

"Yeah, Prez. What's up?"

"You straight?"

"Yeah. I'm straight. What's up?"

"I need you, Clean and Larry to take a trip down towards Laraby Street. The Maniacs may have a bit of information about the drop."

"You got it."

Larry and Clean were already outside on their bikes, waiting for me to get my shit together. When there was business to be done, there were no games played. I strolled up to them and jumped on my baby, heading to the garage on Laraby. The Maniacs had something to say, so we would listen.

"Do you know who fucked up on the drop and let loose?"

"Your President already asked me all this." Guy seemed to be more pissed off than anything that we had shown up at his garage to question him, but Prez must have had something on him to make us come down here.

"I am sure he did. I'm just here to see if maybe we could jog your memory a bit." This was usually Gin's job, squeezing people for information, but it hadn't been since his last major fuck up. Now I somehow had ended up with the task.

"Is that a threat, boyo?"

"Not at all. You of all people should know that I don't need to threaten." I folded my hands under my arms and let my barbed wire tattoo sleeves speak for themselves. If there was someone no one wanted to be questioned by, it was me. I was ruthless. I loved my reputation.

"Yeah, we all know, Wire. No one fucks with you."

"So, tell me what you know about the drop? We are just trying to get to the bottom of this, that is all."

"I don't know shit..."

I rolled my eyes, wishing I could just take him in the back and show him what his entrails looked like. I turned to walk away. If I asked him again and he gave me the same bullshit answer, I may put my fist through his jaw.

"But you might want to check in house," he said almost under his breath.

I turned back around quickly at that. He was crazy if he thought that I was going to let him bash my crew. Not today! "What the fuck did you say?" I took purposeful steps straight toward him. The crew he'd with him all stood up, picking up whatever they could as weapons, and in a mechanics garage, there were quite a few pieces that could do some real damage.

He put his hand in his pockets. He wasn't trying to fight me.

"I'm no snitch, boyo. I'm just saying you are checking with all the other crews. Maybe you ought to check your own. By the way, ain't you missing a man at this interrogation?"

Gin.

He had to be talking about Gin, had to be. Gin's downfall was a little too far and too quick.

Did he set us up?

The more that I thought about it, the more it seemed to make sense. I really hoped not. Gin was a brother even if he was an ass. We'd kill him for this and slowly.

"I hear you," I nodded slowly, looking Guy in the eye. I wouldn't say it aloud, but I wanted to confirm that I was on the same page.

"Fine. Now get the hell out of my shop. Them ugly bikes are scaring away my customers."

"Please, if you want a ride on my bitch, all you have to do is ask!" Clean yelled as he did an obscene dance on his bike. You could always count on Clean to relax a situation.

"Hey, ain't that your visitor's truck? She stalking you or something?" Larry said as he went to start up his bike.

I turned towards where he was looking and low and behold, Keeley's emerald green hybrid truck was parked in a small office building space.

I don't care. Why should I? She means nothing to my brothers or me.

I don't even know when my feet started to go in that direction, but before I could even say anything to Clean and Larry I was already in the middle of the street.

"Guys, give me a minute!" I yelled back at them as I half walked, half jogged towards that truck.

I didn't even wait for an answer.

I circled her car, almost scared that she or Max would pop out, confirming my growing suspicion that Keeley may be stalking me. When I'd gone around the whole vehicle, and she was nowhere to be seen I was a bit upset. Not that I knew why.

I looked inside her truck to see an employee parking pass hanging on the rearview mirror. *Maybe she works here.*

I looked at the building, and if there were any more windows, I would think it was a hospital because of the sterile look of it, but I wasn't too sure about that. There were not many cars and no people walking in or out.

I walked in the door, and a sheepish boy was sitting at the front desk. He nearly shit bricks when he saw me walk in.

"What is this place?" I asked with no preamble.

"Um... ex... excuse me, sir?" Fear, I could almost smell it on him. I looked him right in the face and repeated the question. I didn't like to waste time, and he was wasting mine.

"Oh, this is the Wildlife and Ecosystem Service Station."

What the fuck was that?

"Yeah, whatever. Where is Keeley?"

"Oh, Ms Juric?"

Juric?

"Yes. Ms Juric. Where is she?"

"She is down in the lab. Would you like me to tell her that you're here to visit?"

"I want to see her."

"Now?"

"Immediately."

He blinked a few times. I could see that he was a bit miffed. *I guess this isn't the usual protocol.*

"Shall we get a move on." I gave him my nicest, fake smile as he got out of his chair and slowly led me down some stairs and into a more sterile looking area.

"I can't take you into the lab. They will fire me." He looked up at me. I didn't want the kid to get in trouble. I did see that most of the rooms were completely transparent, glass paneling throughout.

"Is she in an area where she'd be able to see me?"

"Yeah, I think so."

We walked a bit further in, and there she was along with a few of her colleagues, big eye protective goggles on, hair net and full white jumpsuit. It did nothing for her shape. Still, she turned me on.

I walked up and knocked on the glass, jarring everyone out of their little world. I could see the panic on her face when she saw who had caused the disruption.

She excused herself to her colleagues and quickly came through the electronic doors. She got rid of her jumpsuit and ripped the goggles and hairnet off.

"Dillon?" She asked out of breath as she made her way to me.

"Yeah, we need to talk." I had no idea what I was going to say, but I wanted her to talk to me.

She grabbed my hand and pulled me behind her. We walked into an office, and she closed the door behind me.

"Are they outside? How many? They aren't going to come in here, are they?"

I shook my head, I was such a dick. I'd really scared her with that. I know that my club was crazy, but they weren't crazy enough to stalk a woman without cause.

"No, Keeley. There's no one outside. That was just something I said to scare you earlier. I had no idea that you would take me so seriously."

She closed her eyes and took a cleansing breath. She was clearly at her breaking point, and that was my fault. "So seriously? You told me that my life was in danger and that I should watch my back. What kind of person doesn't take that seriously?"

"I know it was a shit thing to do. I didn't think when I said it."

"Tell me about it!" She waved her hand in the air. It looked as though she was trying to throw the conversation behind her. "So, if you're not here to tell me that my life is in danger, what do you want?"

I was at a loss. I was not an apology person. I rarely felt the need to do it, but I knew how I had acted was clearly past the line.

"What's with the fucking attitude?"

Why did I say that?

"My attitude? You come into my life and toss me back into a place that I don't want to be, with a bunch of criminals and lowlifes, tell me that my life is in danger, then treat me like your common corner slut. That's why I have a fucking attitude!" She stepped straight into my space and poked a finger into my chest. "Now, did one of your little club pussies scrape their teeth on your dick or something? You got an emotional stability problem? No, if not, get your shit and get the fuck out my office." I looked her right in the eyes, and there was something about the whole situation that seemed off to me. Then like a fucking blow to the head, I realized what it was.

No fear.

She stood up to me like she would take me out or go down swinging if she had to. No one in my life, not even Clean, would stand up to me for long.

I stepped closer into her space to test her bluff. She didn't move an inch.

I put my hands up in my first ever surrender. Part of me wanted to clap and applaud, but I think that would have just pissed her off more.

"You're right on all accounts. I was a dick. I shouldn't have acted like that."

She squinted her eyes and pursed her mouth. "Was that your idea of an apology?"

I grabbed the back of my neck and began to massage it. Talk about an uncomfortable situation. "Well yeah, I mean… Fuck, I don't know. I've never done it before." I rolled my eyes. This was frustrating as all hell. This was why I didn't deal with women beyond a quick lay.

She shook her head again and smiled a little bit. "Well, usually the words I'm sorry are in there. Then there's some groveling, then some promises to buy me fine wines and chocolates-"

"Nope."

"You're the one who said you wanted to apologize."

"Not that bad."

She laughed now and punched me lightly in the chest.

Wait a minute, is she flirting with me? Is she playing? What's the read on this? I fucking hate women!

"Whatever. Just say you're sorry." She folded her arms and tapped her foot, clearly waiting for me to say the words.

"I'm sorry," I barely mumbled the words; it was like acid on my tongue.

She tsked, shaking her head again. "No, no, no. Say it like you mean it. You have to be genuine or it doesn't count."

If I could hit her up the side of her head and give her amnesia, I would do that instead, but I wanted to be on good terms with her, so I sucked it up and said it again.

I stood up straight and took a deep breath. "I am very sorry, Keeley. I shouldn't have said those things to you. I want you to forgive me."

"What are you willing to do for me to forgive you?"

I smiled at her. "Keeley I am telling you right now unless you are talking about me pulling my dick out and bending you over this desk, you're going to need to be very clear about what you are asking me for."

"Oh jeez, you brute! No, that's not what I'm talking about at all. How about a beer?"

"You want to go out for a beer with me?"

"Well, yeah. Us poor scientists don't have much fun, and you look like you could use a Cosmo or two."

"Hardy har har," I mocked before turning to walk out of the office.

"Was that a yes or a no?"

"I'll see you at eight."

"No, wait. Eight is no good. I'll still be coming in from the field."

I had to turn back around because I had no idea what she was talking about.

"I have to go get some samples this afternoon by Prayer's Creek. It usually takes a few hours. I'll be finishing up around seven, and then I have to drop the samples off here and get home to change for our date. So, like nine-thirty would be better."

I cocked my head to the side. "Date?"

When the hell did that happen? Did I ask her out on a date, or did she ask me? Great. Just what I need.

"Yeah, big boy. It's a date, meaning you have to be on your best behavior. I even expect some damn flowers. Make it happen."

I turned, walking out the door. I had no idea what I'd gotten myself into, and neither did she.

CHAPTER 10

Keeley

"What are you willing to do for me to forgive you?" I asked playfully.

"Keeley, I am telling you right now unless you are talking about me pulling my dick out and bending you over this desk, you're going to need to be very clear about what you are asking me for."

Did he really just say that to me? What a creep. What a sexy creep.

It'd been a long time since I was attracted to anyone, but from the moment Dillon popped up in my backyard, my fantasies had a male lead role. I knew that I came to this small town to get away from all the nonsense and illegal activity that was my father and his people, but something deep inside me couldn't resist a bad boy. Finding his wallet in the house was just another sign that I should pursue this. Since it didn't look like he was going to make a move, I had to do it. I had no problem taking charge.

"Oh jeez, you brute! No, that's not what I am talking about at all. How about a beer?"

"You want to go out for a beer with me?"

"Well, yeah. Us poor scientists don't have much fun, and you look like you could use a Cosmo or two." I tried to play it off as if I wasn't that interested. *Hell, I was so interested.*

"Harty har har."

He began to walk away but didn't answer me. "Was that a yes or a no?"

"I'll see you at eight."

"No, wait. Eight is no good. I'll still be coming in from the field." My colleagues and I thought that a particular species of fish was becoming overly abundant in the freshwater spring, causing a reduction in the population of some of the plant life in the area. Unfortunately, the only time they seemed to be very active was during the early evening hours. Each of us took turns to go. Tonight was my turn, and I honestly didn't want to miss out on the findings.

"I have to go get some samples this afternoon by Prayer's Creek. It usually takes a few hours. I'll be finishing up around seven, and then I have to drop the samples off here and then get home to change for our date. So, like nine-thirty would be better."

"Date?" He seemed a bit confused. *Let me clear it up for him.*

"Yeah, big boy. It's a date, meaning you have to be on your best behavior. I even expect some damn flowers. Make it happen."

My father always told me people treated you how you let them treat you, so if I wanted respect and chivalry, I had to demand it. I didn't care about the flowers, but it was the principal of the matter. If he showed up without the flowers, that meant he couldn't care less about how I wanted to be treated, and that wasn't going to fly with me. If he did bring flowers, then we could proceed further. I would take nothing less than the best. *His best.*

I watched as he walked out of the room, still shaking his head at my audacity. If he stuck around, he'd get used to it.

My whole body was hot. Dillon somehow managed to turn me on with the few words he did say, more than any man before. Sure, I had been in relationships before. I'd given my virginity to another man. It wasn't the man my father had planned me to marry, but nothing lit a fire under me like Dillon.

He was tall, which was a plus since I was already five foot ten. So many men fell from my good graces because they didn't have the self-assurance to walk with a woman that was taller than them.

He was cut, muscles weren't bulging out all over the place like a steroid head, but I swear I could wash my shirt on his abs. The tattoos that I could see seemed to span his whole upper half from his sides to his back and arms, down to his wrist. His neck, face and hands were

WIRE: A WINGS OF DIABLO MC NOVEL

all clean. I remembered when I was helping Clean get him back to the club, and I had this undying need to run my fingers through his hair. It was jet black and unruly. But it was his eyes that stopped me right in my tracks. I could see his whole life story in them. They were dark grey, almost black, and while his face always seemed cool and collected, it was those eyes that gave away all his secrets. I got to him as much as he got to me. He looked at me like I was a piece of meat, and as sexist as it was, I wanted him just to pick me up and throw me over his shoulder.

"Are you finished daydreaming, or should I give you a few more minutes?" Lamonte asked from my door. He was a good friend, but even though he often dropped hints, I was just not interested in him in that way. Too clean cut, I guess.

"Oh, hush. I wasn't daydreaming."

"Sure." He rolled his eyes before he continued, "so, we are just about done here. You remember that you have the late night?"

"Yeah, I'm about to leave now. Did you see anything yesterday in the north quadrant?"

"Nothing extraordinary."

"Darn, I was really hoping we would find the school of fish there."

"No worries. We will find it."

He stood at my door a little longer, obviously waiting for something or wanting to say something.

"Yes?" I asked, hoping to nudge him along.

"Is that guy your boyfriend or something?"

Ugh, here we go.

"No, he is not my boyfriend. We are just friends."

"But he looks like a miscreant."

My eyes snapped to his. *How dare he!* "A miscreant? Why because he wears leather and has tattoos? I can honestly say this is one of the reasons you and I never really hit it off in the dating department. What gives you the right to judge anyone by their looks? Seriously, what year is this anyway?"

He raised his hands, clearly not wanting to agitate me any further.

"I am not judging him. At least, I don't mean to. He seems different

51

from the sort of guy I would expect you to be with. That's all. If you like him and he treats you right, that's all that matters."

"Exactly. Don't forget it!"

Lamonte took that as his exit. He walked out, leaving me to my thoughts and anger. *Why am I so angry?* That was the real question. I think it was because I was so different from what I appeared on the outside. My father was a killer, my mother, a snake. You disagreed with him; he had you killed. You crossed him; he had you killed. You spoke against his name; he had you killed. I grew up around guns, knives, thieves and murderers. These people weren't the enemy to me, they were just people like everyone else. They were just trying to live their lives and they would do what they needed to do to survive and if that meant ending someone else's life, they would do it. I respected a man who could kill for the right reasons. I understood a man that would beat you to within an inch of your life to get any information that may help his family. What I couldn't get down with was the treatment of women. Back where my family was, women were expected to please the man and turn the other cheek when they came back reeking of another woman. They were supposed to be pretty and not cause a fuss. I couldn't do it. I wouldn't be pawned off like a chess piece to smooth over a deal. That, in essence, was the reason that my father and I were at odds. He'd tried to give me to one of his enemies as a show of good faith in a merger that was happening. I'd had no say in it, so I ran off and had sex with the first man I could get my hands on and let them catch me. I would not be tied down to someone unless I was the one with the keys.

I gathered my thoughts and got what I needed to get my samples. It was a cool night, so I bundled up the best that I could.

By the time I left my office, everything was closed up for the night. There wasn't a big crew in this complex so I was used to being alone around this time of night.

I jogged out to my truck, double checking again that I had everything. It was about five pm and it would take me about thirty minutes to get to the site. I was excited to meet up with Dillon later, *maybe find out more about him.* He was a puzzle that I was just desperate to figure out.

I was in my own little world, and it didn't even register I was being followed by three bikes until I got closer to the wooded area. No one went to this side of the creek. It was hard to traverse and there was no real place to set up camp.

They couldn't be from Dillon's crew. He said he was playing. *Who are they?*

I got more concerned when I began to see my turn off, the road unpaved and as far as I could tell, only those that worked at my facility were the ones that would come this way, but the bikes were still on my tail, faces covered and lids off.

I tried to see what was on their kuttes, but they were too far away, and my eyesight was not that good. I could make out one word because it was bigger and bolder than the rest. Chaos.

That wasn't the name of Dillon's club. Wings of Diablo; that was his. So why were these people following me? They hadn't done anything to harm me yet, but I was about to end up deep in the sticks with only one way out.

Time to panic.

No, no. You can't panic. Just go about your business. Maybe, they're going somewhere else.

I pulled into my designated spot and waited and watched as all three bikes continued past me, I exhaled and tried to steady my hands. I was almost sure I was overreacting. I grabbed my kit and made my way to the research site.

The site was about a fifteen-minute trek uphill. I let myself relax against a large tree, my heart still pounding in my chest from the ordeal.

What was that?

Something had cracked behind me. *Was there an animal making its way through the trees?* There weren't any large animals in this area, but I had come across a wolf or two. I was hoping it wasn't that.

I took a quick peek around the tree to see what I was dealing with. Instead of being a wolf, like I'd expected, it was a man. One of the men who'd been following me just a few seconds ago, looking at the ground, obviously searching for tracks. They were looking for me. I turned to the other side as quickly and as quietly as I could manage.

Another man was there, in his hand was a silver gun. This was bad. I had no weapon, no backup and my phone was as good as useless. I had no reception out here. We had said before that we were going to spring for a better phone for the night runs, but we'd forgotten about it and no one had raised the issue again. I could take one of them out, but not three. There was no way that I would win a fight against three armed men. I would have to run.

I waited until I had both of their backs to me, and I took off as fast as I could in the opposite direction. I ran smack dab into the chest of the third man. I hadn't bothered to look for him before I started to run.

"Well, hello there, girly!" He grabbed me around my shoulders and tried to hold me still as I squirmed to get free. "Hey, Scotty. I got her!" He screamed to his friends, who were now closing in on his location.

I reared my head back, flinging my forehead with all the force that I had towards his nose and mouth. When he let go of my shoulders to cup his nose and try to stem the blood spewing from his face, I lifted my leg and kneed him right in the dick. He fell to the ground, hard, one hand on his face, the other on his dick. He wasn't going to get up right away. I continued to run. I could hear them behind me, and I was running into a part of the woods that wasn't familiar. I knew that if I weren't careful I would run clear off the mountain. Some of the cliff faces were shear and gave no indication that they were coming up.

"Come back here, you fuckin' bitch," they bellowed as they continued to run to catch me.

Good, keep talking.

I could use the sound of their voices to figure out where they were so that I could run in the opposite direction and hopefully shake them off my tail.

I turned right and kept running, hoping they would stay on the same path they'd been on a few minutes ago. I pumped my legs as fast as they would go, dodging hanging branches and hurdled downed trees like I was an Olympic runner, nothing like the motivation of death looming behind you to put you to the test.

Then my life flashed before my eyes, followed by darkness and pain. I howled in surprise and agony as I fell legs first down, down, down.

I don't know how far it was I went down, but I hit water and rock when I landed. I bobbed to the surface, raising my face over the dirty stagnant smelling water. I tried to feel for the bottom, but I couldn't reach it. I relaxed and let my head sink under the water and pushed down until I could feel the bottom, but my head was fully submerged. Shit, it was deeper than I thought. I was going to have to tread water until I could figure out a way to get out of here. I put my hand out into the darkness to see if I could feel anything around me. For a split second, there was nothing and immediately, I started to panic, but then I felt a wall and realized that things were as worse as it could get. It was stone and slippery. I was in a well.

I tried to get some leverage but knew immediately, my leg was broken. Even moving it through the water was enough for me to scream out in pain.

I raised my hands and grabbed onto the stones as best I could. I slipped off almost straight away. I grabbed again and again. The force of my motion was enough to suck me under the water. I could feel my heart pounding in my ears. I was dying. I would drown here if I didn't find a way out, but there was no way out. I cried for the first time in years.

"Help!" I screamed at the top of my lungs. "Please! Someone help me!" I sucked in a breath and coughed out the water that came in with it. "Please! Please! Help me!"

I could hear ruffling above me.

"Oh, would you look here, boys," the one they called Scotty said from above.

They all laughed, including the one with the now crooked nose.

"Please. Please help me. I can't get out." I was begging, hoping that I would be able to appeal to their better nature.

"Sorry, doll. That's not happening today. Hopefully, by the time Wire finds you, he'll still be able to tell it's you. I doubt it, though." He shrugged as he stood up and walked away.

I screamed, begging for them to come back. I didn't hear another sound except for my hoarse voice echoing off the walls of the well. I begged God, begged the spirits, cursed Dillon, prayed for him. I just wanted someone to come and help me. The longer I stayed in the well, the more I gave up hope and the weaker I became. I started to feel myself fall asleep and my hand would slip off the wall, sending me splashing down into the water below, waking me for a short time. It wouldn't be too long before I would go to sleep and not wake up.

Wire

I showed up at her house a few minutes after nine-thirty, with some flowers I picked up at the gas station in hand. They were old and only cost $3.99, and I was pissed with myself for actually buying them. Honestly, I only bought them because she still seemed a bit mad earlier and I felt like I needed to make it up to her.

I knocked on the door; no one answered. She couldn't have stood me up because I was a few minutes late.

This is why I don't deal with bullshit like this. I don't have the time.

I wasn't going to knock again. I took the flowers, dumped them in her garbage and was making my way back to my car when I noticed that her truck was not in the drive.

I heard Max barking in the back. I went to the side of the house and unlatched the gate and Max bound out immediately, putting my hand on my gun as a precaution, he sniffed me twice and ran towards my car. It was nearly ten at night and she still hadn't made it home. I remembered she'd said that she had to go to some site near Prayer's Creek. *Maybe she was still at work?* This didn't sit right with me at all. She didn't seem like the type of girl to ignore you when she was pissed. If she was angry at me for being late, she would've called and ripped me a new one. I opened my door and before I could get in, Max jumped in and climbed in the back.

"What the fuck do you think you are doing?"

He just cocked his head to the side and waited for me. I swear if I didn't know any better, I would have been sure that he could understand every word that came out of my mouth.

"Whatever. You mess up my ride and I will leave you on the side of the road. Play around if you want."

The dog leaned down on his forelegs and sat with his head rested on the seat.

I drove back to her job but her car wasn't there either. *Shit is getting really weird.*

I took the nearest road and began to race towards Prayer's Creek. *Where the hell is this woman?*

I pulled off but didn't see her car in the lot. Max hopped out of the car right along with me. I knew which way the creek was but I didn't know what area she would be in. I was hoping this dog was as smart as I thought he was and that he would be able to find her if she was still here.

"Max, can you find Keeley?" He barked once and trotted off into the woods.

I followed behind him but still kept my eyes out for any sign of her. It was night, so it was close to pitch black.

Max ran past the creek, over a walkway and continued going, he'd been here before. I tried to keep up with him but he was moving fast. It wasn't until I heard the damn dog whimpering that I knew that there was something wrong. He'd found her truck, but there was no Keeley inside. It was after ten at night. There was no way that she was still collecting samples or whatever it was that she needed to do.

"Keeley!" I started to call for her. I walked back in the direction of the creek I'd just passed and knew that she wasn't there.

I called for her again but I heard nothing no matter how many times I called her name. Then out of nowhere, Max started to bark and set off running. I didn't know what he'd heard or seen, but I was trusting his senses were better than mine.

"Keeley!" I screamed out for her again as I jumped over trees and dodged branches.

Max stopped a little ahead of me, whining loudly, his eyes trained on the ground. I got to where he was, but I didn't see anyone laying there.

"Keeley!" I screamed again.

"Help. Please." A small voice came floating toward me. I turned around, looking everywhere but didn't see her.

"Keeley, where are you?" I waited for her to answer again and when she didn't, I called for her again. "Keeley, goddammit!"

"Please. Down here."

I looked down, and not three feet from where I was standing was a hole in the ground. I got on my hands and knees, and I could barely see the top of Keeley's head. She was in what looked to be a well.

"Holy shit. Hold on. I'm coming. Hold on, Keeley!" I had nothing long enough to reach her, and no one else was on their way here.

"I'm so tired."

"Stop the shit. I'm here. I'll get you out." I stood up to look around to see if I could use anything.

"Oh, Dillon, please hurry. I can't do it. Please." The small voice coming from the usually fiery woman would have been enough to break a lesser man. I just felt the hum and my muscles loosened up. I was existing in that moment, nothing more.

"Dillon, please!" The shouting of my name was enough to catapult me back to the present.

"I have to go find something to pull you up."

"No, no… No! Don't leave me. Please, don't leave me," she cried.

"I'll be right here. I may have some chain in my car. Just hold on. Max is here. Ok?" I waited until she confirmed that she'd heard me, and then I was on my way. It took me about fifteen minutes to run back to my car.

The minute I was at the car, I pulled out my phone, dialing Clean.

"Speak."

"I need you to get your shit and come to Prayer's Creek, double time."

"Nah, bro. I just got in with a bunny. I'm busy."

"Are you fucking stupid. I don't care who or what is about to suck on your little dick. Get your shit and come. Now!" I screamed down the phone. I huffed as I scrounged around the back of my car for anything that I could use to pull her out of that small space. "Look man, it's a fucking emergency. Keeley fell into this well or some shit. I'm trying to get her out, but she looks seriously hurt. I need some-"

He cut me off before I could even finish. "Keeley's hurt? Why didn't you say that shit before? I'm on my way." I heard him curse whoever was in the room with him out and then loud noises as he made his way out of the clubhouse. I hung up with him and began to run back to Keeley. I'd found a piece of rope, and some chain I used to tie my bike up if I had to leave it in an unfamiliar place and some barbed wire.

I made it back to her in record time. Max was still barking when I laid back down on the ground. She was barely hanging on to the rock above her head. I could see the light slowly leaving her.

"Keeley! Wake up!" I shouted down to her, knocking a bit of dirt on her. It hit her in the face, causing her to sputter, looking up at me.

"I knew you would come. I just knew you would."

"Yeah, princess. I'm here." I tied the rope at the end of the chain and made a loop so that she could put her arms through it. It wasn't nearly long enough, and I was dreading what I would have to do to get her out, but I knew that I had no choice. There was no way that I was going to leave her in there. No way.

I attached the dull barbed wire to the opposite end of the chain, giving it just enough length if I laid down to be able to reach her. *Barely.*

I took off my kutte and my shirt, ripped the shirt in two, and padded both of my hands and wrists.

"Keeley, wrap the rope under your arms," I yelled down to her.

"I can't."

"I don't give a hot damn what you think you can do. You're going to reach up and take the rope and secure it under your arms. Do it now."

She started to cry as she tried to reach up and grab the lifeline above her head. "Dillon, it's too high. I can't reach it."

I could see the distance, and if she reached, she would make it, but she would have to try.

"Stop being a baby. The rope is right there, just give us a little jump, and you'll reach it."

"Fuck you, Dillon!" She screamed at me, snot and tears streaming all over her dirty face.

"Come on, Keeley. Just reach up. I know you can do it."

"Ok... ok. I'll try." I saw the steely resolve in her eyes.

She jumped up once, and the rope missed completely, leaving her submerged in the water. Her little head popped back up as she gasped for air.

She tried again, and this time I felt her fingers graze the rope.

"Come on, Keeley. One more try! You almost got it!"

"Wire!" Clean was looking for me.

"I'm over here!" I shouted over my shoulder but did not move from where I was.

Max began to bark and I could hear Clean running towards the sound. I didn't move, refusing to take my eyes off Keeley and waited for her to catch her next breath so that she could jump up and grab the rope.

Finally, she jumped up one final time, and her hand managed to grab hold of the rope. She used everything she had to get both arms through the loop and under her armpits, now she was just dead weight at the end of the rope.

I wrapped the barbed wire around one hand, feeling the telltale burn of metal slicing skin. I was used to the sensation, but I knew that if I tried to move too quickly, I could do some serious damage to myself.

"What the fuck!" Clean was beside me in an instant. "Oh, shit, is she dead?"

"No, you bastard. I'm sleepy."

I was sure she meant to sound menacing, but it floated up to us as barely a whisper.

"She'll be ok. She will," I said more to myself than to him.

Once the barbed wire was completely up, Clean grabbed the smooth chain with me and hauled her up.

I grabbed her as soon as I could and heaved her out of the well.

She wrapped her arms around my neck and just broke down on my shoulder. I held her as she came to pieces. She shook and sucked in big gasping breaths of air.

"We should get her to the hospital," Clean said from beside me. I looked over her shoulder to see the pain in his eyes. He always did have a soft spot for the ladies, never wanted any of them to cry.

I tried to stand her up, but she refused to let me go. "Clean, unravel the wire from my hands."

The cloth had created a buffer, however, some of the barbs had gone through the fabric buffer I'd created. He'd been doing this for me for years and knew it had to be removed slowly and carefully. I waited until he had freed it all and I put my hands under the frail Keeley, lifting her.

"Clean, take my piece, both of them. I'm going to take her to the hospital, and I don't want to be carrying when I'm with Keeley."

"You got it." He reached against my back and into my boot and took the guns. He would keep them safe for me until I would be able to retrieve them. The last thing that I needed was to get stopped by any pigs while I was carrying.

"Come on, Keeley. We gotta get you fixed up." I looked down at her leg and could see that her ankle was at an odd position. I had no doubts it was broken, none at all. Her hands and forearms were raw in some places from her attempts at climbing up the wall. I felt so horrible for her.

Before I could even make it back to my car, Keeley was already out. She was exhausted.

Clean had his bike so he couldn't take Max, so it was up to me to get him back home and her to the hospital.

I drove as fast as I could.

"Easy cowboy."

Somewhere in between me dropping Max off at their house and speeding towards the hospital, Keeley had woken up, sort of. Her eyes were still closed, but at least she was talking.

"Sorry, I just want to get you there as fast as I can."

"I'd rather get there in one piece, please." She tried to smile. Her dry lips cracked, and she whimpered slightly.

I knew I shouldn't, but I couldn't help myself. "Keeley, how in the hell did you do this to yourself? Are you that much of a ditz?"

"Don't be an ass."

"It's nature, not a choice."

"I didn't do anything. If I hadn't been running from your buddy Scotty, I would've seen the stupid well." She opened her eyes, her glare was unmistakable. She closed her eyes again as I let her words wash over me.

Scotty did this to her? If the Tears of Chaos are after her, she pretty much is a dead woman. This is my fault. Fuck.

I gripped the wheel as tightly as I could, my mind going a million miles a minute. If Scotty thought what I did to him before was bad, he couldn't imagine the pain that I was going to inflict on him this time. Poor Scotty just signed his death certificate.

CHAPTER

11

Wire

"Prez, let me talk to you for a minute." I stormed into the club. I had left Keeley at the hospital. She was having surgery on her ankle. Luckily she hadn't needed any screws or plates in her ankle, she would just be wearing a cast for the next six weeks. The Doctor said she was a very lucky lady. I tried to sit there and wait for her to come out of surgery, but the fact that my rival club was the one to do this to her had me needing to do something. I couldn't just sit there, and I knew that I couldn't retaliate against them without Prez's permission. I wanted that permission and I wanted it now.

"Wire, what the hell do you have on?"

I looked down at my handed down hospital property t-shirt. It was white, so bright the color hurt my retinas.

"Yeah, long day. I want to kill Scotty."

Prez blinked a few times. He was not expecting this type of conversation, especially from me. I rarely had any input into who we were going to take out. However, I wanted this more than anything, and I didn't want to go against Prez's word to do it.

"Don't you think you fucked that boy up enough?"

"No way near."

"Don't tell me this has anything to do with that fucking girl."

I turned around to face my Prez, and with as much respect as I could muster, I said, "This has everything to do with that fucking girl."

"I told you before, don't bring any outside problems into this club."

"And I wouldn't have brought it to you, but the club has brought problems to her."

"What do you even mean by that? What are you talkin' about, Wire?" I could see that he was intrigued by what I had to say. Prez was never someone to turn down a brother just because it went against what the club was doing at the moment.

"That little fuck Scotty and a few other pussies from Chaos followed her to her work site and chased her until she fell into a well. Then they had the nerve to leave her there to die. I know she means nothing to this club, but that woman saved my life. I'll be damned if I'm going to let her be beaten and traumatized just because she was trying to help me. I take any attack on her as a direct attack on me. So are you telling me that I can't defend myself?"

Prez turned around to pace behind his desk. "I can understand where you're coming from Wire, but I know that if you go after him, it'll be full-out war. I have to worry about the other brothers."

I could feel the anger beginning to rise inside of me. I wanted to take action and I wanted to take it now. I was torn between seeking personal revenge and staying true to my club.

"I know I can't keep you from going after that boy, but give me a few weeks to get everything settled, and then I'll make sure he's delivered straight to you" He was throwing me a bone, promising me revenge even if it wasn't right now.

I was never one who needed instant gratification. I could wait to make Scotty scream again.

I walked back into the hospital, hoping that Keeley was either still sleeping or just getting out of surgery. I had so many questions to ask her about what went down, but more than anything, I wanted to make sure that she was truly okay.

It had taken everything inside me to drive straight here and not make a detour to the Chaos Club. It had just dawned on me when I walked in that I had no idea where Keeley was staying in the hospital. I walked up to the administration desk to see if they would give me any information about her and if she was out of surgery.

I stood there for about a minute, and the little girl didn't even bother to look up to acknowledge me.

"Yo!" I called out like she was sitting on the other side of the room instead of right in front of me. If she was going to act like she was blind, maybe she was deaf too.

First, she looked at me like I was a piece of shit, then when she realized I looked like a tasty treat, I saw the lust begin to fill her eyes. Usually, it would take me within fifteen minutes to get her up out of her chair and into a utility closet someplace. However, today I had someone more important to look in on.

"Oh yes, what can I do to help you?" She asked me while she licked her lips, giving me her best 'fuck me' eyes.

A quick fuck would set my mind at ease.

I had to shake the thought out of my head as soon as it popped in. I was pretty sure she was no different from any of the bunnies back at the club. I'd hold mine until I got there.

"Yeah. What room is Miss Juric in?"

"Are you family? A brother?" She asked, almost wishing out loud that I wasn't attached to the woman that just got out of surgery.

"No. I'm not her brother. Yes, I'm family, and that's all you need to know. Now, are you going to tell me where she is, or are we going to continue with this game?"

She seemed a bit disappointed that I wasn't playing more into her flirtation, but I really didn't have the time.

"Yes, of course, she's in room 637."

I turned around before she could even get a full smile out. I made my way toward Keeley's room, and I was surprised to see that she was awake. She was tired though, I could see it in her eyes.

"What are you even doing awake? Shouldn't you be sleeping or some shit?"

"I hate it here. I want to sleep in my own house." She crossed her arms over her chest and pouted, looking the other way.

"Well, princess, you're stuck here for a few days." I tried to lighten the mood. It didn't seem to work for her, though.

"Dillon, don't play. I want to leave." A lone tear fell down her cheek.

Great, now she's crying. What the hell am I supposed to say about this shit?

"So, do you want me to leave, or what's the deal?"

"No, you jackass, why would I want you to leave?"

"Hell, I don't know. You seem upset. Usually, when I leave, things get better." At least, I knew they got better for me.

"No, you leaving is not going to make it better. I don't want to be alone here. The last time I was in a hospital, my mother died. I hate it here."

"Fine. What do you want me to do?"

"You can start by just talking to me, you know, like a normal person." She rolled her eyes and looked away from me. "I mean, if you don't want to stay, by all means, you can leave. Though I wouldn't mind the company."

"I'm good. I can stay here for a little while if you like, but then I got to head back to the club and catch up with Clean."

"Did he come too?"

"To the well? Yeah, he came to help. If I didn't know any better, I'd think Clean has a little crush on you."

"Is that so? Well maybe next time I'll ask him out on a date instead?"

"Have at it." I didn't know what she was trying to pull, but no one was going to get me to be jealous of one of my brothers.

"Ouch. You really don't care, huh?"

"Not in the slightest."

"Well, that's good to know." She turned away from me again.

Does that mean that she does? I hope not. I didn't sign up for that shit.

"So, tell me what happened at the site?" I asked to get her mind on something else besides what we were currently talking about.

"Yeah, well I went to the site like usual but didn't realize they were following me until it was too late. I know better. I should have been looking out."

"Why would you be looking out for the Chaos crew?"

"Not just the Chaos crew, anyone. It's better to keep a vigilant eye than to get caught out there exactly like I did."

"I guess."

"Any way they followed me there and once I saw they had weapons, I took off. They followed, and I fell into the well." She shrugged like it was no big deal. A few hours ago, she almost died because of them. It was a big deal.

"It looks like I have to apologize to you again."

"No, you didn't do this. No apologies from you. Besides, they're painful to hear." She smiled a little.

"Well, they're also painful to give."

"Do we know if they will come back?" She asked.

"I have no idea, but I have a good feeling that they will."

I watched her sigh a shaky breath, putting her hand on her head. She was worried. I would be too if I weren't around, but they weren't going to get to her again.

"I'm not leaving you alone. Not until I am sure they won't be back. Do you understand?"

"What are you talking about? What about the club?" She looked up at me a little bit hopeful.

"They are just going to have to get along without me for a while. Besides, we are all on eggshells right now, we are on the cusp of war, and Prez doesn't want anyone doing anything." I ran my hand through my hair. I wished that we could just end them all, but I guess that was a fight not everyone wanted.

"So what, you're just going to be my bodyguard until they go away? How weak is that." She huffed and crossed her arms again.

"I promise I am more than capable of dealing with any of those fucks." I puffed my chest a little. *Did she think I was a pussy or something?*

"It's not you. I am sure that you could take on the whole army. It's just that I haven't needed a bodyguard for a long time. I vowed never to need one again, and here you are, a new bodyguard. I feel helpless, and I don't like it."

A new bodyguard? What the hell was she into before?

"Well, it's only for a short while, promise."

"You can stay as long as you like." She smiled before she moved on to the next topic.

We stayed in the hospital for three days before she finally put up enough of a fit that the doctor agreed to let her go home if she had twenty-four-hour care. I slept in the chair each of those days, and Clean came over for a few hours a day while I went and showered and stopped by to feed Max. I was feeling totally at ease with her, and she was easy to talk to. We talked about sports, and it turned out she was a big football fan. We talked about movies. I was a big action fan. Finally, she got me to watch some of the superhero crap movies that came out recently, and I found myself more interested than I would have liked. I could get down with Ironman.

She almost ran out of there when the doctor signed the paperwork to say that she was free to go.

"Keeley, slow down. They're going to make your ass stay here if you fall or some shit." She was on her crutches, and she was wobbly to say the least.

"You're right. Where's the stupid chair?"

I pulled the wheelchair up behind her, and she plopped down into it.

"Great, I need you to go sixty straight out the front doors. Let's go. Vroom Vroom."

I laughed at that one. She was a strange girl. I left her parked in the hall while I walked to the desk to see if there was any paperwork that needed to be signed or taken.

"Does she need anything before she leaves?"

The same girl that was there the first day looked at me with those same 'fuck me' eyes. Now she had cherry red lipstick on.

I wonder what that would look like wrapped around my dick.

I didn't shake the thought away this time; I let it sit.

"Dillon, are we ready?" Keeley called out from down the way. Impatient.

"Yes, Dillon, are you ready?" The sound of my name from the girl's mouth threw a bucket of ice water on my lust. I didn't like it coming from her mouth; it sounded ridiculous.

"Paperwork?"

"Yeah, here you go." She reached down and got a few sheets of paper, which I guessed were Keeley's prescriptions circled a few things and wrote a few others down.

She handed the stack to me, and the first thing I saw was her phone number in the corner of one of the pages. She had no way of knowing if Keeley was my wife or something. Some people had no class.

"May I have a pen?" I asked and watched her face light up.

I scribbled on the paper and tore it off and handed it back to her. I turned but not before I could see her face fall into a scowl at the sight of her number crossed out and the words, "Not even with my brother's dick" written down next to it. Maybe that would drop her down a few pegs.

I took Keeley in her new ride and we headed back to her house.

I spent the next few days sleeping in Keeley's guest room. The place was bigger than I thought, and I was glad for that. I had no idea how comfortable that couch would have been. But besides the strange roommate situation that we had going on, we were a lot less close than we had been while she was in the hospital. She pretty much stayed in her room, and I stayed in mine unless she called me. We had meals together but didn't talk about much.

"Dillon, can you come here?"

"For what?" I yelled back. I was watching a movie and really didn't want to move. I had been in a pissy mood since I had gotten here and couldn't figure out why.

"I need you to get something, please. I can't reach."

I sucked my teeth and got out of the bed. *Why the hell would she put something somewhere she couldn't reach?* That was stupid.

I walked into her bedroom and had to stop in my tracks. She had a deep green robe on, soft cotton. My dick sprang to life immediately. She must have just gotten out of the shower. It smelled fresh in her room like washed hair and rain. She didn't even turn when I came into the room, and I could see her on her one good foot tip-toeing in her closet. Her breasts were covered but pressing against the fabric of her robe. I bit my lip as I fought the urge to pick her up and throw her on the bed. I wasn't here for that.

She finally realized that I was in the room with her. "Oh, Dillon, can you get this for me, please? I ran out."

I walked up behind her and saw what she was pointing at, it was body oil, and it was on the top shelf of her closet among about a million girly products. *Why would you need that much bubble bath?*

I reached up from behind her and my cock just barely grazed her backside. I rolled my eyes in pleasure.

What the fuck is this?

I hadn't felt this type of want since I was thirteen years old and I first figured out that if you rub your dick, cum shot out.

"Do you see it?" She asked when I hadn't retrieved it.

"Yeah, give me a fucking second." I was harsher than I wanted to be but I couldn't help it.

"Sorry."

I pulled the oil down and tossed it into her hands. She turned while I was still in that tight space with her. Her robe the only thing that was keeping her body away from my eyes. I looked quickly at the area near her breast, they were still covered so I couldn't see them, but I could definitely see the shape of them. They were large, sitting up, and her nipples looked like they would just cut through the fabric at any second.

"Well, thank you," She said in a breathy whisper.

I looked up to her face. Her pupils were dilated, taking up a lot of space in her clear gold eyes. Her cheeks and neck were flushed.

I have to get the hell out of here. Now.

I felt her get closer to me, her midsection pressed a little harder against my cock and she seemed to be a bit taller.

Is she tip-toeing? Is she going to fucking kiss me? NO!

"You good?" I asked as I backed away quickly. I wasn't going to cross that line with her, especially if I was going to have to stay here while she healed up. Nope, I'm not playing husband for anyone.

She fell back down, flat-footed, the spell broken.

"Yeah, I'm good, Dillon."

"Cool, I am going to wash my ass. Holler if you need anything." I walked out of her room as quickly as I could without breaking the door down. I went back to my room and stripped off all my clothes.

Thankfully the guest room had its own shower because it was exactly where I was headed, I had to get the edge off.

I jumped in and turned the water on to cold. I hissed at the contact with my dick, *just a few seconds and it would go down.*

"Fuck, fuck fuck!"

When a few minutes had passed, and I was still hard as a steel rod, I wrapped my hand around my dick and thought about the last time I'd had sex. It was with Cherry a few weeks ago. God, no wonder I was such a fucking jerk.

I remembered how she danced for me, the feel of her tits in my hand. I stroked my dick hard and fast as I thought about her pussy, taking all of me. The feel of her walls stretching to get all of me in. I stroked harder until I was grunting with effort. Back and forth, inside her tight pussy.

"What the fuck?" I screamed as I punched the wall. Nothing was happening. I had never had trouble getting myself off before, and my cock was still hard and getting painful. Nothing I could remember Cherry doing for me was getting me to the edge. I felt like I was going crazy. I needed to fuck, but I couldn't leave until I got someone to come and take over watch at Keeley's house.

My dick jumped and a bit of pre-cum came dribbling from the slit.

Keeley, this is about her?

There was no way I could go around this house fantasizing about her. But I just needed to this once to get myself under control.

I thought about her in the next room and wrapped my hand around my cock again. I pumped it once, twice and just the visual of her breast in her robe was enough to bring me to release. Not just the norm I do with all the bunnies at the club, but an orgasm that had all my muscles clenched and spasming.

"Holy hell!" I rested against the wall of the shower as I tried to get my breathing under control. I wanted to do that again right away.

I grabbed my still hard dick and began to pump it some more. I was groaning and breathing hard as I thought about her and how gorgeous she was. I wanted to plunge into her honey hole and hear her scream my name. I felt my balls tighten up as another monster release made its way out of me. I bit down on the meat of my hand to keep myself from growling too loud. By the time I was finished, my legs were weak and I was dead tired.

I dried off and sleep-walked to the bed. I couldn't remember falling asleep, but I do remember being completely at ease.

Eight hours later, I woke up fully refreshed. It was pitch black outside, meaning I had slept the entire day away. I walked down to the kitchen area and saw that Keeley was sitting in the living room with a textbook in her lap, Max at her feet.

What is she doing up at this time of night?

A quick glance at the clock on the stove told me that it was almost three am.

"Well, look who decided to join the living," She said playfully. "I have never seen you sleep so much. You are usually up every two hours or so. Are you feeling better?"

"What do you mean am I feeling better? I had no idea I was ill?"

"Well you have been a bit crabby the past few days," She said, looking away from me.

"Yeah, I guess I have. I wasn't sleeping too well. I guess it was catching up on me," I said as I walked over and sat on the couch next to her, careful not to jostle her leg too much.

"How about you? How are you feeling?"

"Much better than I thought I would at the moment. The disability leave is giving me a lot of time to think about my next thesis."

"Your what the fuck?"

She giggled softly and showed me the book and the papers that she had in her lap. "I already have a Ph.D. in Environmental Science but I'm going back to school for my second doctorate in wildlife studies.

"You sure know how to make a guy feel like a dumbass."

She looked appalled. "No. I would never think that about you! You don't need a fancy degree to prove to me that you are smart."

I laughed quickly. "Don't worry about it, princess. I don't offend that easy."

"Oh goodness, thank God."

"I bet your pops is real proud of his little girl."

"Ha! He can't stand it. He thinks the education that I keep shelling all this money out on is useless. He wanted me to stay and join in on the family business." She shook her head like she was upset just thinking about it.

"What is the family business exactly?"

She tutted as she shook her head side to side. "No dice, we always talk about me. Now, I want to know about you. What stories make up Dillon?" She put a fake microphone to my face and I swatted her hand down lightly.

"There are no stories. I am who I am. Nothing made me the way that I am today."

"Impossible. The human body and mind can only become what it is due to the experiences and reactions of its lifetime. You know how to talk because you were taught, you know how to shoot a gun because you were taught, I'm sure you're this closed off because of something in your life that made you believe that this was the way to go. So, spill it." She smiled slightly. "You don't have to go super deep. I just want to know a bit about the man who is basically living in my house."

I don't have to go super deep? Oh, how I want to go super deep, and hard, and fast... ugh.

I shifted in the seat, hoping that my train of thought wasn't enough to have me tenting my pants.

"Fine."

"Great!" She sat straighter in the chair, waiting for me to start. Problem was, I had never really talked to anyone about anything super personal before. Everything was very superficial with the folks that I knew. Clean may have known a secret or two and maybe Prez but that was it.

I guess she must have seen my hesitation. "How about we start with playing twenty questions? You only have the option to pass three times, if the questions are too personal for you, so choose your passes wisely." She squinted her eyes at me playfully.

"Whatever. Let's just get this over with. I'm getting tired already."

She laughed and clapped her hands together. "Ok, so do you have a close relationship with your parents?"

"Nope, they're both dead." That was easy.

"Oh, I am sorry," she said, the joyful look on her face now replaced with guilt and sorrow.

"For what? Did you know them?"

"No, of course not, but it's hard to lose parents, I know."

"Yeah, not mine. They were assholes," I said matter-of-factly.

"Ok. Next question, um… How old were you when you lost your virginity?"

"Ah shit. I don't remember. It was so long ago."

"Is that a pass? I mean this is one of the easy questions." She put her hands on her hips and pouted a bit.

"Wait, let me think on it."

She hummed the jeopardy song, and part of me wanted to put my hand over her mouth to get her to shut up.

"Ok. I remember. I was thirteen."

"Thirteen! What the hell were you doing having sex when you were thirteen?"

"It was at the club. It was one of my first parties."

"Oh wow, you have been with them for a long time."

"Yup, since I was thirteen."

"I don't remember seeing any children in there the last time that I was there."

"Nope, it was one of the bunnies daughters. She was seventeen."

"Oh snap, and with an older woman. I bet you rocked her world."

I had to laugh out loud at that one. "Actually, it was the complete opposite. I came once before I even touched her, and when she got me cleaned up and I finally penetrated her for the second round it was done in like three minutes. I was so spent, I fell asleep still on top of her. In fact, fucking is the only way I get any good sleep."

"That can't be true. You had some good sleep today and unless you have been sneaking women through my windows, there was no sex going on in here."

I guess fucking my hand with thoughts of you on the brain is just as good.

"Yeah, today was different." I shrugged hopefully, she would let this question drop.

"Ok, what is your favorite thing to do?"

"Ride."

"Your bike?"

"Yeah, I feel so free when I'm on my bitch. She always takes care of me."

"I'll have to get a ride with you one day. Sounds very relaxing."

"We'll see." What she didn't know was that I'd never had any women on my bike. They could hitchhike for all I cared. My bike was special to me and I wasn't going to have any random chick's twat funking it up.

"Why were those other bikers trying to kill you?"

Fuck, here comes the hard stuff.

"I'm the club's pain manager, and we messed up the wrong person due to some bad information. I really messed the kid up, and he wasn't even the one we were after."

"Scotty?"

"Yeah. How did you know?"

"He looks like he's on the mend, but you can tell that he's... well he's different."

"And he will be for the rest of his life." I shrugged and blinked at her a few times.

"Did you want to hurt him?"

It sounded like she was questioning my loyalty to my club. That was something I just wouldn't stand for. "I'll do whatever the fuck my club needs me to do. And if that means that Scotty has to go, then Scotty has to go."

"I understand that, but if it was just you and him on the street, no directive from anyone, do you Dillon, want to kill him?"

My head was thumping, I couldn't understand the question. I didn't know what she was asking of me. "What the hell are you talking about? I just told you I do whatever is I need to do for my club."

"You are not your club and your club is not you. Don't you realize they are two separate entities?"

"Of course, I fucking realize that. Don't talk to me like I'm a kid."

"I'm not. I am just asking if you can make your own mind up without instruction from the fucking club, and from what I see here, you can't."

She was pissing me off, big time. "Pass!"

"Fine! Brunettes or blondes?" She screamed the question at me.

I smirked a little. "Why are you yelling hair types at me?"

"Shut up. You are so infuriating." She laughed and re-asked the question, softer. "Do you prefer brunettes or blondes?"

"I like women, all women."

"So, anything gets you up and ready to go, huh?" She raised an eyebrow, almost like she didn't believe me.

"Well, I do prefer if a woman is natural. I am not a fan of the over-sized breasts and ass that everyone seems to be in love with nowadays. And I would prefer it if the woman had a bit of meat on her. I don't want to grab you and be worried that I am crushing your lungs."

She nodded. "Well that is different. Most men like fake tits."

"Not as many as you think."

"Ok, next question. Why do you always seem so afraid when we get close to each other?"

Ah shit!

"Pass." I wasn't even going to argue about it.

"What the heck? That was an easy one!" She screeched at me.

"I don't have to answer it even if it is easy."

"Fine." I could see the wheels turning in her head. "Do you find me attractive?"

"You're a woman. I already told you I like women. Why are you asking me about things you already know the answer to?"

She opened her mouth, but no words came out.

"Are we done here? I think I'm going to go back to bed and see if I can get a few more hours in."

"No, wait, just a few more questions."

"This was a bad idea."

"Why? You scared?"

I squinted my eyes and crossed my arms over my chest. She was pushing me. "Hurry up and ask your goddamned questions so I can go the fuck to sleep."

"Don't be a dick."

"Just nature."

"Do you have any feelings for me?"

"Pass."

Shit! That was my last pass. Hopefully, she'll forget. I should have answered that one.

"That was your last pass." The cheshire cat grin broke out on her face. So much for hoping she would forget how many passes I had used.

"Do you want to make love to me, Dillon?" She asked, and it was barely a whisper.

Fine, she wanted to take it there, let's take it there. "No, I want to fuck you, hard. So hard that you are screaming and shaking in my arms."

Her eyes and her mouth were wide open. "Oh."

"Yeah. Oh."

"So why-"

I stopped her before she could ask what she was going to ask. I already knew what it was going to be. *How come I had never made a move.*

"I don't know how long I am going to have to be here with you, but I'm not leaving until the threat has been cleared. I ain't looking for an ol' lady. I would just fuck you and toss you to the side like the used whores at the club. I didn't peg you for someone who would go for something like that."

"You're absolutely right, I'm not okay with that at all, especially since I am no one's used whore." She bit her lip and looked away.

I stood up, ready for this conversation to be over. My dick was getting hard again, just thinking about fucking her even if she just told me that what I was able to give her and what she would accept where two very different things.

She stood up as well but wobbled slightly. I reached out to catch her before she went down.

She clung to my arms as she steadied herself. She looked up at me, clear want in her eyes. She moved in a bit closer and her hands caressed my arms as they made their way up towards my neck.

"Keeley, stop. I don't kiss. It doesn't do anything for me." I spoke but for some reason the words sounded soft, without conviction.

"I don't think anyone has shown you tender before, Dillon, can I just try?" She whispered.

I shrugged.

I had kissed a few women in my past, and it was always spit and biting. It was nothing I liked, just a smushing of faces. I never saw the point.

She pressed her body to mine. On her tip-toe, she was nearly as tall as I was. She ran her hands up my neck and into my hair. She was gentle, so gentle. She stared into my eyes and I stared right back into hers. There was something in them that I'd never seen in any of the bunnies. I couldn't place it.

She pulled me down slightly and kissed me softly on the cheek right at the corner of my lips, her lips felt like feathers on my face, plump and soft. She brushed her face with mine, her nose barely skimming mine as she moved to the other side of my face where she placed another kiss, equally soft. Her hands were knotted in my hair, but there was no tension, she was just holding on to me, breathing me in. I looked at her face and saw the want, the flush of her cheeks as she hesitated, moving towards my lips. I felt her breasts rubbing on my chest with each one of her breaths, slow and steady. This wasn't my usual because she was worshipping me. She wanted me to feel what she was feeling, and for the first time, I really was.

She kissed me just as lightly, on my mouth this time. At first, I didn't even react, just let the contact sear itself onto my brain. She did it once more, and everything in my body woke up. I had to touch this woman. I had to kiss her. I wanted her more than anything, but I couldn't get my body to move. I was stuck.

"Do it again," I said. The gruff growl that left my mouth caused her to inhale and rise back up on her good foot, kissing me on my mouth, just a bit harder this time.

My arms wound around her waist, and I kissed her back once. Then again and again. She was so sweet; the air around me sparked and crackled like it was on fire. I had never felt anything like this before, and I wanted more of it. Immediately.

I could feel her one leg begin to tremble, so I picked her up and wrapped her legs around my waist, her sweet spot was hot and damp, hovering just above my cock. I would do anything to rip off the little pajama bottoms she had on so that I could bury myself in her, but I couldn't get carried away. *I couldn't.*

"What the fuck is this?" I groaned as I kissed her again. The taste of her mouth set my whole body on fire. I just couldn't get enough. Before long, she was clawing at my shirt and I had her pinned up against the wall as she ground herself down on my dick. She wanted me bad, and I wanted her. I was getting to the point of no return. If I didn't stop this soon, I would be buried to the hilt in her honey pot.

She arched her back slightly, and the movement caused her to slide down directly onto the head of my dick. The heat, the wetness and the fact that I was on at least a three-week dry spell had me groaning, tensing up like I was going to bust my load in my pants like a fucking teenager.

I have to fucking stop, or I am going to regret this.

I tore my face away from hers, dragging in great big gasps of breath as I wrapped my arms tighter around her waist to keep her absolutely still.

"Why are you stopping?" She tried to pull my face back to hers.

"Don't!" I locked my neck, keeping her from pulling my face to hers.

"Why?"

"I already told you, I can't give you what you want, and I won't," I said finally, looking back to her.

She looked hurt as she began to unravel her legs from my waist. I set her down gently and waited until she was stable before I backed all the way away.

"Why can't you admit you like me? What's it going to hurt?" She asked, the telltale wetness now around her eyes. She was about to cry.

"Like you?" I barked out a fake laugh. "What makes you think that? Because you got my dick hard? No princess, I just want to fuck and you throwing yourself at me is making it hard for me to do what I gave my word to do." I stepped back up close to her and let the fury that had somehow replaced the lust come spewing out. "I'm here for business and nothing else. I owe you a favor. Once this shit is over, you can get the fuck out of my life. You and that sweet pussy." I smirked at her.

"Oh, is that so?" The tears were streaming down her face but her eyes were strong, and her posture looked like she meant business. "Well, you can get the fuck out of my house. I don't want any favors from someone like you." She looked at me like I was worse than the dirt under her boots. "And as for my sweet pussy?" She continued, stepping closer to me so she could whisper in my ear, "that little taste you got on the wall, is the closest you will ever get to it." She backed away, staring me straight in the eyes. "Now go back to your club. I am sure the bunnies miss you, Wire."

She just reamed me out. I was stuck between being pissed off that she would even think to talk to me like that, turned on that she did, and feeling like a straight up pussy that all I could get was the mandatory snatch from the club bunnies, this had gone so far left. But I think the part that hurt me the most was the fact that she called me Wire. It was a first, and I actually hoped that she never did it again.

"Whatever. Fuck this." I grabbed my kutte and my boots from the door and was out of there before she would ever be able to tell that she'd affected me, but she had. Even as the wind whipped past my face on my bike, I could still feel her lips pressed against mine.

God, I want more.

CHAPTER 12

Wire

It had been three days, three fucking days since I last saw Keeley. I had sent a few brothers on rotation to make sure that no one was messing with her, but I hadn't stepped anywhere near her since that day.

I sat in the clubhouse and watched as the bunnies danced around the men. There was a party going on, but it was nothing too big. I wasn't even looking at any of them. I'd gotten a maximum of ten hours of sleep in the past three days. I just couldn't get the way she felt on me out of my head or the way she said my name or the way she kissed me. It was all just stuck in there, and nothing that I did to get her out did the trick.

"What the fuck are you thinking about? Lez has been trying to get your attention for the past five minutes." Clean slapped me on the back of the head slightly, jarring me from the constant daydream of Keeley.

"Don't fucking hit me." I glared at him like he was one breath away from a beat down.

"Jeez, what is the fucking problem, Wire?" He glared right back at me.

"What are you hitting on me for?"

"That girl is over there popping her pussy basically right in front of your face, and you're not paying her any mind. What did your dick stop working after you left Keeley?"

I stood up, one more word and I was going to have to punch Clean in his fucking face.

He raised his hands, backing down.

He was right, though. I had come down to this party to get my dick wet, and as it stood right now, all the good girls were going to be gone before I had a chance to get one. I had to put my game face on.

I focused on the girls remaining. Cherry was already gone, Lez and Marie too. Those were my normal go tos. I did see another girl there that would've usually caught my eye. She was short, and looked like all of her parts came from god and not the plastic surgeon. She looked clean, and I hadn't seen her humping all over everything that was walking. I sat in a chair and signaled her over. She walked over slowly like she was trying to seduce me. I had no time for that shit.

"Hurry the fuck up, cupcake," I called out, and she put a little pep in her step.

She turned to face me and began to dance, putting her hands in my hair and pulling hard. I wrenched her hands off me. "Turn around."

She did, instantly and began to grind her ass on me. I waited for my dick to respond. And I waited... and waited. Nothing. This was a problem.

She was putting her all into it, flinging her head back, sucking her fingers, playing with her snatch. No matter what she did, it was like I was watching it from someone else's body. I wasn't feeling any of it.

She hopped up on my lap and really started to put her all into it.

"Oh shit." I heard Clean say from behind me, and it wasn't an 'Oh Shit' like the new girl impressed him, it was an 'Oh Shit' like we got problems.

I turned to see what he was looking at.

Oh shit!

I threw the girl off my lap to the floor. "Shit, my bad," I said to her as I tried to get up and run towards Keeley, who had snuck up on me and was watching this girl give me a lap dance.

"What the fuck, Wire?"

"My bad, I didn't mean it. You good? Are you hurt?"

"Nah, I'm good."

I left her there on her ass as I rushed towards the door where Keeley had just hobbled out.

I rushed out the door, past Clean and Larry. "Keeley, hold up."

"What the fuck for? You're obviously occupied." She continued to walk away the best that she could on her crutches.

"Keeley, just fucking wait," I called out again as I managed to grab her arm and turn her around. Her face was red, and her breath was coming fast and hard. "What the hell are you even doing here? Is everything alright at the house?" Maybe, Scotty had shown up or something.

"What do you even care, Dillon? Just let me go."

"What? What is this?" She was so angry. Why? "Hold on. Are you fucking jealous?"

"You know what? Yes. Yes, I am fucking jealous. At least I'm woman enough to admit it! Here I was thinking I was too much of an ass to you, and you're in there getting your dick rubbed on."

"What does that matter? You ain't my woman, Keeley. I can have my dick rubbed on by whoever the fuck I want," I said, trying hard to keep my cool.

"You're right." She took a deep breath, trying to calm herself. "You are so right. I'm not your woman. I am nothing to you."

"Look, I didn't mean it like that, ok? You do mean something to me." I looked at her, putting a tentative hand to her waist and pulling her closer to me. This was the closest I'd been to her in the past few days, and just touching her like this was enough to ease my mind, even if just a little. I hadn't realized how on edge I was until I touched her.

"Dillon, I understand that you're not with the whole boyfriend and dates sort of thing, but I won't lie and say that I don't think about you more than I should. I want you to be ok, that's it. I'll back off."

That was the last thing that I wanted. I wasn't a fool; I wanted her even if I shouldn't.

"You're right. I don't do the boyfriend thing, ever, not at all. But I don't want you to go away. I've never felt like this for anyone, and it's pissing me off. That kiss was-"

"It was amazing. I felt it too." She pressed herself against me, and just her proximity was enough to get my cock up and raring to go.

"Yeah, now what the hell am I supposed to do with that information? You don't fit into my life. I need to keep that in mind, and so do you," I said as I backed away from her slightly.

"Dillon, I get it. All I'm asking is that you don't shut me out. I liked our talks and since I'm pretty much stuck in the house, I don't have anyone to talk to. Maybe just come by and visit once in a while. No pressure." She looked up at me, hopefully.

I looked into those clear gold eyes determined to say no to her, to tell her that I wouldn't do that, and it was best if we had a clean break. But the word 'no' would not form on my tongue. "Alright, I can do that. I'll stop in from time to time to check on you."

She smiled brightly. "Great. See you soon." She turned to walk towards her car. "Oh, by the way, I hope that girl gives you syphilis, and your dick rots off." She continued walking toward her car, not giving me another glance.

I laughed. I wasn't expecting that. "Oh, what the fuck." I was already having a hard enough time focusing on the women in the club, nothing was going to happen tonight. I turned and walked back into the clubhouse, passing Clean on my way.

"That girl is going to be the end of you."

"What the fuck did you say?" I turned back to Clean. He'd been getting more and more ballsy as the days passed.

"Bro, out of all the people in this club, I'm the one who has had your back the longest, knows you the best, I promise you, you will not survive that girl."

"I guess it's great you don't have to worry about that then."

"If you think this won't be bad for everyone, you're dead wrong, Wire. You're dead wrong." He walked past me and caught up to the short girl that had been grinding on me earlier. This party was over for me. I had Keeley on my mind and only Keeley.

CHAPTER 13

Wire

Three weeks pass, and I had kept my promise to Keeley, visiting her every other day. It had been difficult, but I had to admit that I was in a far better mood after I came home from a visit with her. We hadn't kissed since that first day, and though everything in me wanted to do it again, I wouldn't admit that to her. I was the one who put myself in the fucking friend zone, and now I had to stay there.

"Wire, you heard anything from your girl lately? Any of the Chaos brothers shown up?" Prez asked as we all sat to discuss the club's next steps. We'd had a few of the shops that our club provided protection to get broken into and destroyed. We had a feeling that it was Chaos, but they weren't taking the blame for it.

"They drove by a few times, but the brothers were there, so they kept moving," I answered. They were still tormenting Keeley, but she didn't let it faze her in the least. She kept her head high, going about her life. If I didn't know any better, I would think that she thought that the Chaos crew wasn't even a threat to her. I loved her confidence.

"Alright, have you spoken to the Misfits?" He asked Clean.

"Yeah, they're down with us. Chaos has been taking prospects from them, so they have no love for Monte and his crew."

"Ok. Larry, I am going to need you to go find out where the Outlaws stand. And Wire, you go find out if the Wolves would be down with us. We need to know who is on our side and who we need to be on the lookout for."

"Wait a minute. What about me?" Gin asked clearly miffed that he'd been passed over, especially for an intel job.

"Gin, your ass is benched until this whole shit with Scotty is behind us. You got a problem?"

"Nah, Prez. We all good." He was glaring at Prez like there was beef. That was a big no, no. We all got up and crowded around Gin.

"You're looking at me like there is a fucking problem. You sure you're good?"

He looked around, seeing that he was about to get his ass beat by everyone in the crew for disrespecting our Prez, a contrite look took over his face. He knew better.

"No, Prez. I'm with you."

"Good. You all know what you have to do, but be careful when you ride. Shit is getting thick out there. Don't get dead."

With that, we moved out and went about our tasks.

I took my bike out and rode to the Wolves. It was a stressful meeting. Some clubs were squeaky clean and only did events if it had to do with community building, and then there were clubs on the other side of the spectrum like the Iron Wolves who'd kill you in broad daylight if you even looked at them the wrong way. They were reckless, and they didn't like the other crews. I tried to feel them out in the meeting, but for all I knew, they could be against us or with us. We would just have to find out when the day came if it ever came.

I was so busy going over the meeting in my mind that I had almost missed Keeley's truck parked on the side of the road. I had to stop and do a U-turn to get to where she was parked.

She was outside? How come no one told me that?

I looked into the little bar that her truck was parked in front of, and there she was sitting at the bar, in a pretty top and shorts, her feet in bright pink glittery flats, both of them. I hadn't even realized that she was getting her cast off. *I guess everything went well with that.*

I opened the door to the bar, and the dull sound of people laughing and glasses clinking on the tables made me smile slightly. Then my entire world went silent and numb as I watched the man next to her grab her around her waist and hoist her up from the stool. His hands were on her, and she was laughing. I hadn't even realized that I was still walking over to them until I was ripping her out of his hands and punching him right in the face. He went down with one punch, letting out a squeal.

"Dillon, what the hell?" Keeley screamed at me, beating down on my back. I was going to pick him up and hit him again, but he was still on the floor, whimpering.

"Dillon!" She shouted out again and began to pull at me.

I turned towards her. "And you talk about me! Fucking hypocrite!" I shook her off and stormed out of the bar.

"Dillon, wait!" Keeley yelled, still running behind me. "Dillon, you're going to make me break my ankle again. Just fucking wait!"

"What Keeley? I don't got time for this shit. Go back inside."

"No, god damn it! Fucking talk to me. What the hell was that?"

I took a deep breath. I was pissed, beyond pissed, and I didn't even know why. I just didn't like that man with his hands on her.

"You come pumping all this shit about how much you think about me and how jealous you are, but you're up in there on another man's dick. What the fuck is that about...?" I stopped when I saw that she was laughing. It was soft, barely noticeable except for her shaking shoulders.

"Are you jealous?" She asked as she walked carefully up to me.

"No, I'm not fucking jealous. I don't fucking do jealous."

"Aww, Dillon. Come here."

"You think this shit is funny?" She was pissing me off more and more. I just wanted to get on my bike and ride.

"Yeah, I do actually. Can you come over here please?" She put her hand out and waited for me to join her. I did but only because I wanted to touch her, no other reason. If this was the last time that I was going to touch her, I wasn't going to deny myself. She turned in my grasp, so her backside was pressed against my front. We were now both looking through the glass window of the bar.

"Look over there. Do you see the guy you just punched in the face?"

I looked around her head, and he was just now getting up off the floor. The fact that he was stable again made me want to go back in there and punch him again.

"Yeah, so what?"

"Now, do you see the man helping him up and wiping him off?"

"Yeah…"

"Well, that's his husband, Dillon."

Husband? He's gay? He wasn't hitting on Keeley?

I let out a long groan and dropped my head to Keeley's shoulder as she laughed at me harder now. I'd misread that whole situation. They were all just goofing around.

"We were out celebrating me getting my cast off and me going back to work next week." She stuck out her once broken ankle and wiggled it around a bit.

"Shit, I fucked up."

"Yeah, just a bit, and since I like this bunch of friends, you can go in there and tell them that."

"What? You must be out of your mind."

"I'm not. You just walked in there and punched my friend for no reason. Go apologize." She turned around and faced me with her hands pressed tightly to her sides.

She looked up at me, and the biggest part of me wanted to tell her to fuck off, but the part that wanted her to kiss me again won out. "Shit!" I stormed past her, walking back into the bar.

I made quick work of getting back to where the little party was. They all began to back away as soon as they saw me approach.

I raised my hands to show them that I meant no harm, at least this time around.

"Look, that's my bad," I said as I looked at the guy that had previously been on the floor. "I saw Keeley in your arms, and I thought that you and her had a thing, and I just lost my shit. I shouldn't have done that."

"Oh, you like Keeley?"

"Ah, it's complicated."

"That doesn't sound too complicated. You like her enough to go into a jealousy fueled rage, and from the big ass grin on Keeley's face over there in the corner, she's into you too. Where's the complication?" One of the other women in the group asked.

I turned and saw that Keeley was indeed smiling like a little girl in the corner as I made my best apology to the man I had knocked out by accident.

I looked at the semi injured man again. "You good?"

"Yeah, I'm alright. Nothing seems to be broken. You owe me a martini, though," he said, giving me a slight smile, but he didn't move any closer to me. He was keeping his distance.

I nodded and walked over to the barkeep. She was a friend to the Diablos. "Listen, put that whole party on my clubs tab under me."

"You got it, Wire." She smiled up at me. I had fucked her once before. She'd cried when I kicked her out.

That got a few hoots and hollers from Keeley's friends. Free booze always changed the mood.

Keeley had walked up behind me and addressed her friends. "Everyone in one piece over here?"

"Yeah, your boy toy over here just picked up our whole tab!" The woman said, raising her now full glass in the air.

She laughed and wrapped her arm around my waist. "Well, guys, I need to get some rest so I can be back on a working schedule by next week."

"Sure!" They said mockingly, and it seemed like they thought we were going to leave and have sex.

If only.

"Whatever guys. Thanks for the party. I'll check in tomorrow." She turned, and we began to walk out of the bar. "Crap!" She hit herself in the head and turned back towards the bar. "Hey, you have my keys."

The barkeep just shrugged. "Yeah, can't give them back. You've had about four drinks already, and you haven't been here long enough to sober up."

"How do you expect me to get home?"

"Cab?" She said as she continued to wipe down the bar.

"Don't worry. I got her." I said and turned Keeley towards the door.

"Wait. What am I going to do about my truck?"

"We have to leave it, princess. We can come back tomorrow for it."

"But someone could mess with it." She was very concerned about her truck, it seemed.

"I promise you no one is going to mess with it."

"Ok, well, let me get a cab."

I rolled my eyes at her for being so ridiculous, then I realized what I was thinking and almost laughed at how right it all seemed to fit in place. "I'll take you home."

"On your bike?"

"Yeah, unless you're too afraid." I saw the steel resolve solidify in her eyes. She didn't like to be called a wimp.

"I am not afraid. I've just never done it before, that's all."

"It's not that hard. Just let me lead. All you have to do is enjoy the ride."

"Ok let's do it. I'm tired."

I hopped on my baby and instructed her how to get on behind me, telling her to be careful of the exhaust. She could get a wicked burn if she touched it with her leg. Before I knew it, we were off and on the way back to her house.

"That was so much fun!" She hopped off the bike with an ease that I was impressed with.

"I am glad you liked it."

"I loved it! I may buy one of my own."

That was a sexy thought, Keeley on a bike, riding next to me on the open road.

We walked in, and I grabbed her waist, pressing her back against me. Having her riding on the bike with me, with her arms wrapped around me, had turned me on. Not to mention the fact that it had been close to two months since I last got laid. None of the club bunnies could keep me interested anymore. All I wanted was Keeley.

"Hmm, someone has missed me."

"Yes." It was all I could say, and it was so true. It hurt.

She turned around, pressing herself against me. She tiptoed, raising up and getting closer to my face. "Do you want me to kiss you again?" She asked, unsure if it was what I wanted. It was, and as much as I didn't want to admit it, I was thinking about that kiss more than I was thinking about being buried deep inside her.

I nodded without taking my eyes off hers. Keeley reached up, running her fingers through my hair. That feeling alone was enough to make me want to rip her clothes off. I had to kick the door to keep my focus. She bit her lip, before kissing me on the cheek. Then she trailed feather-soft kisses towards my neck and ears. She readjusted and switched to the other side, kissing my other cheek. I could feel my breathing become erratic. I was losing control. I wanted her so bad, and the feeling of her tight, soft body worshiping mine was pushing me way over the edge.

Finally, she kissed me lightly on the mouth, and everything in me broke. A feeling of electricity shot through my body, and I groaned as I lifted her off the floor, causing her to wrap her legs around my waist. I swung us around and crushed her to the door, slamming my lips back down on hers. I kissed her like she was hiding my last breath in her mouth. I couldn't get enough.

"Oh, Jesus, Dillon."

I growled in my chest at the sound of her whispering my name. I focused my oral assault on her neck. I liked to feel her squirm on me.

She grabbed my hair harder this time, pulling me back towards her face. She kissed me deeply and was able to arch her back so that her sweet spot was right on my cock. My knees nearly gave out when she started to grind down hard on me. She was trying to get off. I could hear it in her breathing.

I grabbed her ass with both my hands, still keeping her up on my waist, but now I was pressing down. Her movements were becoming jerkier, and her grip was slipping from my neck.

"Dillon, oh please. I… oh… I'm going to fall," she whimpered into my mouth, her pitch beginning to rise. I turned us around and moved us quickly toward the couch. I dropped her down.

"No!" She reached for me, wanting her release. I looked at her, a wolf looking at his prey.

I grabbed the satin shorts she was wearing, and with one deft move, I ripped them off her body. She gasped and her eyes dilated a little more. This was caveman 101. Most women liked it when a man dominated them. I watched as she reached up and took her top off, leaving her bare breasts for me to admire, her pale pink nipples hard and peaked just waiting for me. I moved back over her, letting my hand settle on her mound.

"You been waiting for me, Keeley?" I asked her as she tried to get my shirt off.

"Why are your clothes still on?" She dodged my question.

I pressed down harder on her clit with my palm and let one finger play with her opening through her panties.

Her hands dropped as she felt what I was doing.

"Dillon…" My name was a plea, she was begging me.

"I asked you a question. You been waiting for me?"

"Oh god, yes. There's no one else. No one."

"You going to remember that?" I pulled her underwear to the side and put one finger into her sweet honey hole while my palm still applied pressure to her clit. Her breath started to hitch.

I wasn't going to wait for an answer this time. "You're so fucking tight, Keeley, I can't wait to bury myself inside you."

"Yesssss!" Her hips had a mind of their own now. She was pressing down right at the edge of her release. I could feel it in the tension of her legs.

I stilled my hand right as she started to hold her breath.

She tried to move her hips to get the last bit of friction she needed, but I held her tightly, completely still.

"What are you doing to me?" She opened her eyes slightly, her words only a whimper. I kissed her hard again and began to move my hand fast and hard against her clit. Her whole body started to shake as she screamed into my mouth. Breaking the connection of our mouths, she ripped her mouth from mine.

"Oh my god. Oh my god. Dillon, I can't… argh…" She jerked and bowed off the couch. Right as her pussy began to release my finger, signaling that her orgasm was almost over, I curled my finger and began to massage her g-spot, causing a whole new set of spasms to run riot through her canal. "Oh shit, what are you doing?" She screamed and began clawing her nails down my back. I wondered just how many times I could make her come back to back like this from clit to g-spot back to clit.

"Oh, you're going to kill me. Oh, but it feels so good, Dillon." Her

WIRE: A WINGS OF DIABLO MC NOVEL

head was whipping back and forth. She grabbed my hand and stilled me. I guess she was at her limit. We would have to raise that limit. I was far from done with her.

She grabbed my shirt.

"No."

"What, are you crazy, you can't work me up like that and then say no." She was pissed off.

"I can't give you what you want, Keeley. We spoke about this already."

She turned her head and thought about it for a minute. I wanted her to tell me the fuck with all the rules, that she didn't want me to be her boyfriend or her man or whatever she just wanted a no strings attached fuck.

Please just say you want to fuck, for fuck's sake.

"You're right." She pushed me up and got off the couch, pacing in front of me with nothing but her panties on.

I was going to bust right there in my pants just from looking at her. I was in pain.

"But hands and kisses are still fair game, right?"

Was she looking for an out, fuck that she could have any out she wanted if that meant that she would keep on fucking touching me.

"Yeah, I'm down with that."

"Good." She stalked back towards me and straddled my lap. She ran her hands through my hair and began to grind on my already hard dick, and I stopped her. I was past the point of a lap dance, that shit fucking hurt.

"Oh, poor baby. Let me help you with that," she whispered in my ear as she lightly ran her tongue down the curve of it. My hips bucked up at the sensation.

She pushed her hands down my chest and abs, using her pinky nail to scrape along the top of my pants from side to side. The feeling was so intense that I almost came from that right there.

"Keeley, stop fucking with me!" I grabbed her hair and pulled her back to me, kissing her roughly, desperate to get off. Now.

She used her free hand and undid my belt before unzipping my pants. Thankfully I wore boxers, so it was easy for my cock to spring free once we got past the belt and the jeans.

"Can we enjoy each other's body without fucking?" She asked, looking at me desperately.

She wants me naked? Shit, I'm down with that.

"Yeah, no fucking. I got it." She pulled my pants and boxers off. My shirt came off in almost the same second.

I let her straddle me again and realized just how difficult this was about to become. She had taken her panties off, leaving her completely nude in front of me, only an almost sheer strip of hair on her pussy. My dick was nestled up against her stomach, the warm juices from her pussy dripping onto my lap. All I would have to do was lift her, and I would be able to bury myself inside her.

Fuck, fuck, fuck. I need her on me now!

She kissed me again. This time with more passion, if that was even possible, her hands pulling my head back so she could get better access. Her hand then went in between her legs, and I could feel her playing with herself. I pulled back so I could watch.

"Fuck, you are so damn sexy."

She smiled, her eyes hooded with want as she moved her hand from her pussy. She wrapped those same dainty fingers still wet and glistening with her juices around my throbbing and hard cock.

"Oh, fuck," I dropped my head back against the couch and closed my eyes tightly. I wasn't ready for the pleasure I was feeling from just her touch.

"You have to tell me what you like. I want to please you." She kissed me again and began to pump her hand. "Let me please you, Dillon."

"You're perfect, Keeley, so fucking perfect." My hips bucked up again. I wasn't going to last long. "Princess, this is going to be quick. I want you so bad."

"Cum for me, Dillon. I want you to," she whimpered again.

My balls tightened as shots of lightning began to gather, starting from my hamstrings, going to my lower back, and just when I was about to blow my load, she stopped her hand, gripping tightly at the base of my dick, stopping me from coming.

"Keeley, what the fuck are you doing? I need to fucking cum."

She looked me in the eyes. "I know…" She began to raise herself off me. I pulled her back down on me roughly. She must be crazy if she thinks she's going to leave me with this case of blue balls. She kissed me. "Trust me, Dillon." I let her arm go. I would do whatever the hell she wanted right now. "Close your eyes. Relax." I hoped she wasn't about to do some kinky shit, but again, I would do whatever she wanted. I did what she asked, and the minute my head hit the back of the couch, I could feel her drop in between my legs, her warm, tight mouth wrapping around my dick. I nearly jumped straight out of my skin.

"Oh fuck!" I grabbed her head, and she took all of me in, only gagging slightly as my cock pushed down her throat. I didn't even have to coax her. The stopped orgasm I was about to have a couple of seconds ago came rushing back with a force I had never felt before. She was sucking and moaning on my dick, and I was fucking speechless until that first spark crashed behind my eyelids.

My eyes popped open as I watched her work. I was gone.

"Keeley, I'm going to nut. Fuck."

She didn't stop. In fact, she doubled her efforts. She wanted me to come in her mouth. *I think I could love this fucking woman.*

I roared as the orgasm screamed through my body, "Fuck!" I clenched every muscle I had. She nearly sucked the soul out of my body.

I felt my body relax; it was the best orgasm I'd ever had.

"Well, was it ok?" Keeley looked up at me, wiping her mouth.

Are you fucking kidding me? I think I saw Jesus.

I couldn't say that. "Yeah, that was good."

She smiled and crawled up on the couch with me, laying her head on my chest. I was asleep before I could even begin to say anything else.

Clean was right; she was going to be the end of me.

CHAPTER 14

Wire

I spent the next few weeks going between Keeley's house and the club, Chaos club was still off the grid for the most part, but we were still having issues with our properties and shit going missing. I knew that it would only be a matter of time before this blew up, and we would have to fight.

I was waiting for it.

Keeley was back to work. Loving the time that we were able to spend together, she had kept to her word. There was no pressure. Sometimes, we would just talk when I came over, and sometimes she would suck me off until my toes curled. Surprisingly I was good with either option.

I parked my bike in her drive and walked up to her door. Using the key she had stashed in the plant pot by the door, I just walked in.

I kicked my shoes off in the corner and went to find her. She usually met me at the door, but today it looked like she was in the back of the house. I made my way through the house and saw her standing near her back door, looking out the window.

I grabbed her shoulder to turn her around.

She screamed and swung her arm. It was only by chance that I saw the sunlight glint off the blade and had a chance to move out of the way.

"Oh my god, Dillon!" She dropped the knife and threw her hands over her mouth. She was shaking her head from side to side. I could hear her mumbling, "I'm so sorry, so sorry, so sorry..."

"What the fuck, Keeley!"

She dropped down to her knees and began to sob. She looked broken. This was new to me. This girl was usually as hard as nails, and I hated to see her cry.

"What's wrong? What happened?"

"Nothing, nothing. I'm ok." She tried to calm herself, wiping the wetness from her eyes. I wasn't buying that shit.

"Bullshit. You're having a whole fucking fit right now. What's wrong?"

"It's nothing. It's silly."

"What's silly?" I wished she would just tell me and get over it.

"I thought someone was out there last night, walking back and forth. Max has been on edge all night, growling and barking every once in a while." She shrugged. "I thought I saw them in the back by the other house, so I grabbed the knife in case I wasn't hallucinating or something, and then you walked up behind me. You just scared me is all."

Someone was outside? What the fuck?

"Why the hell didn't you call me?" I moved her to the other side so I could look outside.

"It's probably nothing. I can't be sure that anyone was there. Maybe Max was barking at a squirrel or something."

I stared her down. She couldn't be that dumb. "Does Max normally bark at squirrels?"

She put her head down. "No… I just didn't want to keep bothering you."

I tried to soften my approach. Grabbing her head gently, I pulled her lips up to mine, kissing her softly. "Nothing you can do is going to bother me, but I need to know if you are in danger. How can I protect you if you don't tell me?"

The steel resolve snapped into place. "I can protect myself, you know. I'm not a poor helpless damsel."

"I agree. That swipe and scream technique would have taken down a big motherfucker." I laughed lightly as she play punched me in the gut for making fun of her.

I kissed her again. I was getting used to kissing her whenever I wanted. I liked it.

"Let me just go check this out. Ok?"

She bit her lip and ran her hand to the small of my back, and she felt the gun there. She nodded and let my arm go. She wanted to make sure that I was protected.

I opened the door.

"Max!" She called out behind us. He trotted up towards me. "Štiti ga." He stood right in front of me, and every step I took, he trotted right alongside keeping up.

I had no idea what she'd said, but I trusted that dog to keep her safe. If she sent him with me, then I was sure he would keep me safe too.

I walked to the back of the house, and there was nothing there besides her concrete backyard and a small array of patio furniture. I walked to the side of the next house that was only cut off by a small fence. I peered over and saw a bunch of cigarette butts and what looked like piss in a puddle on the side of the next house. She wasn't crazy. Someone was watching her house.

Fuck!

I looked down the alley to see if they were still hiding out anywhere, but based on the peel out rubber on the ground in front of the other house, I assumed they left when they heard me coming in.

I rushed back to Keeley, suddenly not wanting to leave her alone even for one minute.

She was standing there, waiting for Max and me to come back. He trotted up and sat down right at her feet.

"You're not crazy. Someone was out there."

"Really? Are you sure?"

"Yeah, I'm sure." I shook my head and took out my phone to text Clean. I had to stay here with her. "I think we're going to lock it down for a few days."

"What? What does that even mean?" Her pitch began to rise, a clear sign of rising emotions.

"I mean, you're stuck in the house with me until I say it's all clear."

"No," she said defiantly.

"I'm sorry. It wasn't a question. That's what is happening. So either you get down with that on your own, or I tie you down, and you still have to stay here."

"You would do no such thing!" She fisted her hands at her sides.

"Watch me," I said as calmly as possible. I would do whatever I had to do to keep her safe, even if that meant making her my prisoner.

I could see the gears turning in her head as she walked over to me and put her hands on my chest.

"Dillon, I can't just stay locked up in my house." She ran her hands through the hair in my nape softly. "I have a life. I have a career that I love, and I can't run to the closet every time some big, bad man decides to try and scare me a little bit. I'm not built that way."

Say no. Tell her she can't go. Say she has to stay in the house where it is safe. Oh, you fucking pussy!

"Fine, I won't lock you in." I was becoming a real marshmallow when it came to her. She only had to rub on me or kiss me, and I was practically putty in her hands. She knew it too. "But you will have someone, more than likely me, with you wherever you go. You go to the store to get fucking tampons I'll be holding the basket."

She opened her mouth to argue, I could see it on her face, but I guess she realized that this was one of those fights that she wasn't going to win.

"Fine, but only until the threat is gone. Correct?"

"Yup."

She sighed and smiled at me. "You drive one tough bargain."

"Yeah, and you are too difficult."

"Well, I don't know. I was always taught, the harder the work, the better the prize."

I just groaned in response. She raised herself up on tiptoes and kissed me softly on my lips. Grabbing her neck, I deepened the kiss, and I could do this all day long. I pulled her shirt out of her pants and put my hands on her skin. I bit down on her lips just to feel her squirm and moan in my mouth. She began to rub her hands over the growing bulge in my pants, and I pressed her against the wall so that I would get more pressure. All this petting and kissing and shit was going to drive me crazy. I hadn't been without sex this long since I was fucking thirteen and started having sex.

"No, no no. We have to stop."

"What the fuck? No." I wasn't even hearing what she was saying. If this was all that I could get, I wasn't going to be denied.

"Dillon, I have to go to work. I need to be there at a certain time."

"No, you don't. It's Saturday."

"I do. I promise I do." She pushed me away again.

I grabbed her ass hard and squeezed.

She squealed and kissed me once more, softly on the lips. "You want to come with me?"

"You don't have a choice in that matter, do you?"

"I guess I don't. You're so damn bossy." She walked over to the door and slipped on her hiking boots. I slipped on my biker boots and we walked out.

Keeley had to go to the forest instead of the office today. Apparently, there were some samples that she needed to pick up that one of her colleagues set out yesterday. I was watching her work and could see how focused she was. It was as if I wasn't even there. I liked to see her in her element. Finally, after about two hours of watching her pick up vials of water and label them before putting them in her cooler, she turned to look at me.

"Hey. Do you want to see something cool?" She looked up at me, and the excitement was clear on her face. I didn't have the nerve to tell her no.

"Sure."

"Great, come on. We have to hurry, the sun is almost setting."

She pulled me in the opposite direction. It was almost a jog. We made it to a partially cleared area in the woods, where there was a small lake. We sat down on the edge of the cliff and looked down at the lake and the trees.

"Ok, watch this." She sat in between my legs on the ground, and we watched as the sunset. It was beautiful, one of the most beautiful sights I had ever been forced to watch in my life. I hugged her too my chest and watched the magnificent view. It was made even better because she was there with me.

"One day, I want to get an environmentally sound cabin or cottage in a place just like this, where there's peace and nature all around me. No guns or anything. Just peace."

Peace, I could get used to that. I could get used to a life of peace with her.

I pulled her tighter to me and watched the sunset with this woman. *How did this happen?*

CHAPTER 15

Wire

We got back to the house around seven that night, but before I could even properly get out of the truck, I could see that there was a problem.

"Why is that guy standing in front of my door?"

It was a prospect from my club. Both Clean and Prez both knew that I wasn't going to leave Keeley by herself, and since it wasn't Clean or one of my other brothers that had come here to relieve me, Prez must need all hands on deck.

"Come on, we have to go." I pulled her around the car and went straight to the prospect.

"What's going down?"

"I don't know anything Wire, but Prez said that you needed to get back to the club ASAP." He was one of the newer prospects, but I could tell that he had heard about me. I could see the fear.

"Alright, look, you watch out for this woman with your life." He nodded once and waited for her to come towards him.

"What is going on?" Keeley asked, clearly rattled by the new face at her door.

"I am not sure, but I will have my phone on me the whole time if anything goes down, hit my jack."

"I can take care of myself, Dillon."

"Stop the shit. Do what your fucking told, and that's it." I wasn't about to have her try and fend for herself when there was something potentially big going on.

"Fine, Dillon. Keep your freaking pants on. I'll behave." She smiled slightly.

"Prospect, I mean it. Don't let her out of your sight. If something happens to her on your watch, you have me to deal with."

"You got it, Wire. I'll be on point."

I grabbed her arm and pulled her to me hard. "No fucking around."

"You got it, babe."

Babe, did she just call me babe? Why am I smiling?

"I'll be back as soon as I can."

"I know."

I walked into the club, and there was no music playing. The bunnies were away, and I could hear Prez shouting in the church.

"Wire, where you been, bro?" Clean ran up behind me and clapped me on the back.

"I was with Keeley. What happened?"

"Chaos retaliated. They got one of our prospects. They said that it was payback for Scotty."

I sighed. I knew that I'd only done what I'd been instructed to, but somehow, all this mess seemed like it was my fault. I was the one who messed Scotty up, and I was the one they were coming after. Now one of the young prospects had gotten into the line of fire, so much pain for a simple misunderstanding.

"Shit, did they kill him?"

"Nope, they cut off his legs and hands."

"What the shit?"

"They wanted to make sure that he would never ride with us. Never."

"Fuck."

I guess I could understand, but taking away someone's ability to ride was torture. It was something that I would do.

"Yeah, tell me about it."

"So, what's Prez thinking?"

"I don't know, they're still having church. From what I can gather, he feels that this closes the issue, and any further problems mean war. We got three brothers missing right now, so if they don't show or we think The Tears of Chaos had anything to do with harming them, we're going in guns blazing."

"I hope they have the balls to fuck with us, I really do. They all need to be taught a lesson."

I went up to my room and tried to relax until the verdict came down. I wanted this over, right now. I could hear pieces of what was being argued about in church but not enough to get my hopes up. One thing that I did hear a lot was that they were thinking about disbanding Gin. They were going to take his patch. That was almost as bad as the torture. To be accepted into the brotherhood and then kicked out, it was almost impossible for people to adjust back to a civilian lifestyle. I did not envy him in the least.

I laid back, waiting for the next shoe to drop. I checked my phone every so often, in case Keeley called. But I wasn't prepared for what came next.

There was a loud sound of metal scraping on the concrete floor outside. I jumped out of bed and grabbed my piece, ready for whatever was going down.

I slammed open my door and nearly ran straight into Clean. "What the hell was that?" He had his gun ready as well.

Everyone in the club was armed and either running or walking towards the door. Prez and the rest of the higher-ups must have heard all the commotion while they were in church because they were coming out as well with their weapons in hand.

Before anyone could make it to the door, it burst open. Guns were drawn, but luckily no shots fired. It was just the two brothers that were missing. But they were dragging an enemy member with them, a young prospect from the Tears of Chaos.

Magic looked pale and seemed to be bleeding from a wound in his chest. I was no Doctor, but chest wounds were never good.

"Shit. What the fuck happened?" Prez ran past all of us to assist them. Clean helped Larry hold the Chaos prospect, who was gagged and bound at the wrists. He was fighting to get free.

"This fuck ran up on me and stabbed me. No preamble. No fight. He just stabbed me," Magic said, blood still pumping through his fingers.

"Get the Doc down here!" Ryder, our treasurer shouted, jumping in with Prez to get Magic situated.

Prez handed him off to a prospect then turned back to Larry.

"Has he said anything?" He nodded towards the still squirming prospect.

"Nope, he got a lot of fight in him, though."

"That's ok. We got someone who can get the fight out of him. Wire, you're up!"

For a second, I hesitated. It was the first time I had ever hesitated when Prez asked me to interrogate someone, but all I could hear was Keeley asking me that dumbass question.

Did you want to hurt him?

This prospect looked young, almost too young to be in a club as ruthless as the Tears of Chaos, but here he was chomping at the gag and kicking his legs like he was going to take me down if he could.

"Find out what the deal is, why he attacked Magic, and if Monte has anything planned that he knows of."

"To what means?"

"What the fuck does that mean?" Prez looked at me like I had three heads. I had never asked that before.

"I mean, look at him, Prez. He's young. Where do you want me to stop?"

"Wire, you don't stop until he has no more information." He looked at me hard, waiting to see if I had anything else to say. I didn't. I would do my job.

I looked over to Clean and Larry. "Set him up in my studio, chain him to the table." I walked past everyone, going up to my room. My chest was tight, and I didn't know why, but this felt so wrong.

I gathered all the gear I would need to do the task, just like I had done countless times before. The splatter guard, the gloves, the rubber overalls, in case I needed to involve some water or there was excessive blood, but no matter how much I went on with my regular prep, my chest still felt like it was going to implode.

I sat on the edge of the bed to get myself together and could see that my hands were shaking.

"What the hell is this?" I balled my hands into a fist and released them, shaking them out a bit. I did this over and over until I had that under control.

I grabbed my gear and made my way to the studio. The sweat was pouring down my face before I even made it to the prospect.

I opened the door and could see that he was squirming on the table, cuffed tightly, his hands above his head, and his legs spread and pulled taut.

"I'm here to gather information from you, we can do this the painful way, and you will tell me what you know, or we can do this the not so painful way, and you will tell me what you know." I always started with the same spiel.

"Fuck you and your bum ass club."

I pulled out my ball-peen hammer and hit him hard, once, on his fifth right rib. I hit him hard enough to break the rib but not hard enough that it would pierce the abdominal cavity. I didn't want his lungs to collapse before he could even tell me anything.

He screamed out in pain but said nothing I wanted to hear.

I broke two more ribs and moved on to the other side. He screamed. He didn't stop screaming, but I didn't stop until it looked like he was having a hard time breathing.

The tightness in my chest and the sweat that was dripping off my brow was now long forgotten. The hum had already settled into my muscles; this was what I was meant to be doing. Death and destruction.

"Let's start with a simpler line of questions. What's your name?"

He wheezed and took in a deep breath, the broken bones hurt with every movement he made. "My name is Kenneth Purcell."

"How old are you?"

"I'm seventeen."

Seventeen? What the fuck? I'm torturing a goddamn baby.

The hum that had previously washed over me started to lift, and I could feel my chest begin to tighten again.

This shit was just wrong. It was so wrong, but I had no choice. I had to do it for my club for my brothers. I was beating this little boy for some information that he probably didn't even know was important.

I calmed my breathing down and tried to force down the rock that had somehow managed to settle right down on my chest.

Why the hell am I feeling like this? Am I having a heart attack?

"What the hell are you doing here at this age?"

"That's none of your fucking business. You won't get me to snitch on Monte."

The hum began to descend back on me fully.

"You don't even know what you're fighting for, do you?"

A glob of phlegm infused spit landed directly on my cheek. "Fuck you," he wheezed out.

I grabbed my mallet and swung down with all my might. I barely registered the fact he was screaming and crying now, both of his ankles were broken and pointing in awkward directions by the time I'd finished.

"Why did you stab Magic?"

"Had to," he said in between sobs.

I had put a knife to sit in a flame at the beginning of the session. I pulled it out of the flame and stuck the white-hot metal object against the thin skin on the bottom of his feet. At first, he tried to kick, and then the begging began. I left it there until his skin melted around it, holding the blade in a loving melted caress. It would continue to burn until he had no nerve endings left in his foot.

I looked at him expectantly. I rarely asked the same question more than once. I was giving him another chance to tell me why he stabbed Magic.

He got the hint. "Monte told all of us that the Wings of Diablo were our number one enemy, and if we were able to take out any of the brothers, we would automatically get patched. And we would get all the benefits. I'm just tired of sleeping on the fucking streets. So yeah, I saw the fucking kutte and I didn't care who was under it. I just wanted to be in the crew so that I could sleep better."

"Monte and your crew already avenged Scotty. So what's the plan now?"

"You think I'm a dumbass? If I tell you, they'll kill me."

"You think you're in a good position to hold out?"

He groaned. I was done with this game. I picked up a cricket bat and attached the barbed wire to it.

"Wait, wait. You don't understand. I can't tell you. I can't." Everyone knew my expertise with the barbed wire. I could skin you alive and never nick one artery. I was a fucking savant when it came to dealing out pain with it.

I raised the bat, slamming it down on the skin of his abdomen. He screamed but didn't answer the question. Slowly I pulled the board, carving deep rivets into his body, long strips of skin rolling upwards, blood spilling over his sides. I took his nipple off with this strike. He was hyperventilating by the time I raised the board over my head again to deliver my next blow.

"He wants... he wants... he wants..." He stuttered through the pain, but he was trying to tell me something.

"Hurry the fuck up, or this is going to get worse."

"He wants to take out this entire chapter. He thinks this whole town should be his. He already has recruited the Wolves to help him out, and a few other crews are working together to take all of you out. They are going to pick you off one by one. I swear that's all that I know."

I believed him. I walked down to where his feet were still cuffed up and ripped the knife that had melded to his flesh off. There was no muscle left, and I could easily see the bone, blackened by the heat of the knife and the burned skin from above and below where the knife had been.

I washed my hands and walked out of the studio like it was just another day in the park. If he said anything after that, I couldn't hear it. I didn't feel my hand open the door to let me outside. I couldn't see the people around me. I walked straight up to Prez, who had a few of the higher-ups with him and told him what the boy told me. It looked like he said 'good job,' but my ears couldn't hear it. I just turned on my heels and went to my room.

I took all of my clothes off, got into the shower, and let the hot water wash any remains of that boy's blood off my body.

CHAPTER 16

Wire

I laid in bed. I wasn't sure for how long, but it wasn't until the flashing lights signaling that my phone was ringing caught my attention that I moved.

It was Keeley.

"Speak."

"Eww. I hear your asshole hat is firmly planted on your head this evening."

"What do you want?" I blocked out what she said. It wasn't any information that I needed.

"Why do you sound like that?"

"Keeley, I'm busy."

"Busy with what, Dillon?" I could hear the uneasiness in her voice, but my name on her lips began to break through the fog. It was like she was reaching out to me, and the only thing that I was able to grab onto was the sound of my name in the wind.

"I just… They brought him here, and I had no choice…" The large stone that was once in my chest began to make its way back, and I rubbed at it, thinking that it may go away with pressure.

"Come over."

"I just want to lay down."

"Come over now, Dillon." She hung up on me.

I looked at the phone like it was the one who offended me. I put my boots and kutte on and dragged my ass to my bike.

I couldn't even tell if it took a few minutes or a few hours to get to Keeley's.

She opened the door before I could even push the bell.

"Oh my god. What the hell happened?" She pulled me inside and grabbed my face lightly. She kissed me on the cheek, the eyes, my head, everywhere she could reach. She looked back to my face and could see something, but I wasn't sure what it was.

I was opening and closing my hands. They had started to shake when I got off my bike. The tremors seemed to make their way up my arms and into my chest. It was suddenly way too hot. I pulled my kutte off and pulled at the collar of my shirt, trying to get a bit of a breeze.

"It's so hot. Why the fuck is it so hot?" Sweat was pouring down my face.

The stone in my chest seemed to get bigger. I was having a hard time breathing around it. I took deeper breaths, but for some reason, the same amount of air wouldn't come back out.

What the fuck is happening to me? I'm dying; I have to be dying.

"Dillon, what's wrong? Talk to me."

"I can't breathe. I'm dying." I slid down her door, still trying to catch my breath and get my body to stop shaking. My peripheral vision was getting dark, and I could only see what was right in front of me.

"Babe, you're not dying, you're having a panic attack. You're ok. I promise you're ok."

I'm having a what? Bullshit!

"Look at me. Focus on me. Now take a deep breath in."

She mimicked what she wanted me to do, and I followed her. My lifeline.

"Now, let it out." Again another demonstration and again, I followed.

We did this a few times, and along with a few kisses and some petting from her, I was able to come back to my senses.

I was a big ass man. I'd been shot, stabbed, and in numerous car and bike accidents, but I'd never felt any closer to dying than I had just then.

"Does this happen a lot?" She asked tentatively.

"No. It just started happening today."

"Why?"

"How the fuck am I supposed to know?" If I knew what caused it, then I would've taken care of the problem."

"Something caused it, Dillon. When did you first start noticing the symptoms?"

"Don't play fucking doctor with me, Keeley. I'm good!" I got up and stomped over to the couch. I felt like such a wuss.

"I'm not playing doctor. I just want to help. Maybe if we know what triggered it, you could get a hold on it quicker next time."

Next time? This is going to happen again?

"How do you know so much about it?"

"I used to have panic attacks all the time. It was one of the main reasons I had to leave my father. I couldn't deal."

"They brought a prospect from the Chaos crew. He had stabbed a brother, and they were able to catch him and bring him in." I couldn't believe that I was telling her. This was supposed to be club business, and no one else was supposed to know.

"Did you know him?"

"No. I had never seen him before, but he was so young. Only seventeen years old. He stabbed Magic because Monte has declared open war. If the boy had killed Magic, he would have been patched, no questions asked, and he would have gotten all the perks."

"Perks?"

"Being in a Club is more than just a hobby, it's a community, a way of life. He would've had a job, a bed to sleep in, food to eat, a family. That's why we're so committed to these clubs, they're everything to us, it's everything we are."

She just nodded like she understood.

"But when Prez told me to get the information out of him, it just felt off. I don't know."

"It was wrong."

"Yeah, I guess. I still had to do it, though." I shook my head, feeling the guilt of beating that boy weigh heavily on me.

"Will he live?"

"Yeah, he's going to have a hard time walking, and he will have some cuts and scars but nothing that'll kill him."

She nodded. "You have to protect your family, no matter what. I will never say that I agree with you beating up that boy, but I understand why you did it. The fact that you reacted like this, so violently, means that you have a soul somewhere beneath that hard skin. You're human, Wire. If you didn't feel some of this guilt, I'd be worried about you."

So, this shit is what normal people feel like? I can't stand it.

"This is your fault."

She scrunched her eyebrows, clearly not understanding.

"This was the first time in all my time with my crew that I asked myself if I really wanted to hurt that boy. Apparently, the answer was no."

She smirked a little bit. "Well, I guess I'm rubbing off on you a little bit, sorry it was this extreme."

"Tell me more about your father."

"Ugh. I'd need a lifetime to explain him."

"I'm not going anywhere."

"Fine." She rolled her eyes, "His name is Marko, and he's a bastard. I know he loves me and I love him, but I just can't deal with all the violence. There is no talking. There is no right or wrong. It's just simply kill or be killed with him."

"Do you still speak to him?"

"Every once in a while, he checks in to find out if I'm still living and breathing, to remind me that I can disrespect his name even here."

"Disrespect him?"

"Yeah. He had decided I was to marry someone he had chosen. It wasn't someone I loved or was even attracted too, so I had sex with the first guy I could find and made sure they both caught me in the act. Essentially I was exiled after that, but there are still things that I can do way over here that would piss him off enough to come and teach me a lesson."

Teach her a lesson?

I didn't like the sound of that at all.

"Well, let's not do anything to piss him off."

"I try all the time." She shrugged and looked over at me, running her hand in my hair. "So why did you join the Wings of Diablo?"

"It was an easy choice. It was either stay with my dick head stepfather or join the Wings."

"Your parents were that bad to live with?"

"Yup, it was non-stop drugs, fucking and beatings. The last time I was there, he'd punched three teeth out of my mother's mouth, and when I tried to intervene on her behalf, she beat me with a frying pan, so I ran away. I had no money, no clothes, other than what was on my back. I tried to steal from the President of the club at the time. He caught me, and when he threatened me, and I didn't break, he began to use me for small side jobs. I got better, but it wasn't until I was about nineteen that they figured out that I was pretty immune to doling out pain."

"What do you mean you are immune?"

"Well aside from today, I usually go into a numb like state when anything crazy is going down. For some reason, the only thing that has ever been able to break me out of it, besides time, is when you call my name." I shrugged like it wasn't a big deal.

She smiled and planted a kiss right on my lips. "Awww, you like me. You really do!" She joked with me.

I rolled my eyes and ignored her. But I did, I really did.

"What the hell?" I woke from my sleep and could feel Keeley straddling me on my stomach. We'd spent the entire day together and had a wonderful time. I'd gone to the market with her and picked up dinner, and we'd watched a movie and made out before we fell asleep like we usually do. Ever since the day we agreed that we'd be able to be in each other's presence naked without having sex, we hadn't slept together clothed. Everything was good when we went to sleep, but now she was staring at me, looking like she was about to cry or kill me, possibly both. I saw both my guns still on the nightstands. They were a little too close for comfort.

"Keeley, what are you doing?"

"What is wrong with me?"

"What?" I didn't understand. *What is she talking about?*

"I just don't understand."

"Tell me the fuck about it. What is your problem?"

"Don't you fucking curse at me, Dillon. You're pissing me off." She slapped me hard on my bare chest.

Yeah, she's going to kill me.

I run through the day in my mind, trying to think of what I could've done or what she could've seen that would piss her off. I was coming up with a big fat blank.

"What is wrong with me?" She asked me again.

"There is nothing wrong with you. Why do you keep asking me that?"

"Then why am I not good enough?"

Oh, wait… this can't be what she's going on about.

"What makes you think you're not good enough?"

"The fact that you still haven't made me yours!" She punched me in the chest this time.

"Woman, we spoke about this. I can't give you what you want."

"Why not?"

Another hit. "Look, I'm not going to lay here and be beat on. Get the fuck off me so I can leave."

"Why not?" She asked a bit softer. "Talk to me. Tell me what's stopping you from being with me."

I shut my mouth and just looked to the side. I had my reasons, and I wasn't going to be questioned by her. I didn't break that easy.

"You aren't going to talk to me?"

I just stared and rolled my eyes, she was getting on my nerves.

"Ok, then let me give you a little incentive to talk to me." She raised up on her knees and grabbed my face, kissing me. She kissed me deeply, letting all her passion flow through. I loved the feel of her lips on me, and the argument was quickly forgotten after just a few seconds.

What the fuck? No, no, no… Yes!

While she was kissing me, she somehow managed to lift up enough to line the head of my cock up with her honey pot. I was already as hard as a rock, a common affliction whenever I was in her presence. She sat down on me but only slightly, the head barely parting her lips.

I could feel the warmth and wetness, though. I could feel the plush satin of her walls straining to keep me out.

"Don't move an inch, Dillon, or I will get up and you can leave."

"What the fuck? What are you talking about?"

"Why can't you be with me?"

"Keeley, are you shitting me right now?" It had been months since I was balls deep inside someone, and all I had wanted since then was Keeley.

"Tell me why." She swirled her hips so slightly that if I wasn't so sensitive right now, I wouldn't have noticed.

"The fuck, Keeley! I swear on my life if you don't stop your shit!" She didn't understand the desperation, the blind need that had just overtaken me to grab her hips and slam her down on me. It was carnal, a need stronger than fight or flight, stronger than hate or love. I needed to be inside her. She was playing way too close to the fire for her to leave me like this now.

"Oh, you want me to stop?" She sunk a few millimeters further on my dick. The only thing my brain could think to do was raise my hips off the bed and move further inside. I knew she was serious about getting up if I moved though, in the back of my mind, I wondered if I could get off in one pump.

"Tell me why." She swirled again.

I wanted to cry, it felt so good, and I was so frustrated with her and with the situation. I grabbed on to the headboard and tried to block out the sensation. She was torturing me, plain and simple, and I was so close to breaking, it was pitiful.

"Dillon, please," she whispered to me. I roared in frustration, my desperation at an all-time high. I wanted her, and I wanted to be with her, I wanted to make her mine.

"If something were to happen to you, I'd fucking kill everyone."

"You think you'd be putting me in danger?"

"I know I would. You don't belong in my world. It's full of killers, fighters and fucked up bikers. It's not for an angel like you."

"I'm not worried about anyone else but you. All I want is you. All I need is you." She swirled again, dropping a little more. The whole head of my cock was inside her now. Her walls began to clench around it, and her face and chest began to flush.

"All I want is you," I said to her, pulling her head back to mine. I already knew that if anyone was ever going to be ol' lady material, it was her. I just wanted to keep her away from the dirt. But I had already sullied her and she was fine with it.

"So, take me, Dillon. Make me yours."

"You don't know what you're asking. I'll never let you go."

"It's all I'm asking for." She raised her head slightly, her hair creating a curtain, blocking everything from my line of sight but her face and chest.

I felt my resolve crack at that very moment. I grabbed Keeley by the legs and flipped her underneath me.

I plunged in halfway before her hand shot out reflexively to stop me. "You're mine. I take what's mine when I want it."

She smiled at me, her eyes hooded with pleasure. "Go in slowly, babe. I want to feel you stretch every inch of me."

I threw my head back, willing myself not to cum from her words alone. I let myself dive deeper, inch by glorious inch until I was snuggled inside her tight warm pussy. I didn't move after that. I couldn't. I was sure if I did, I would find out if I could indeed cum in one pump. The answer was a resounding, yes!

"Dillon, please. I want you so bad. Move."

"Give me a second, Princess." I pulled out slowly and could feel her walls contracting around me, not wanting me to leave.

"Fuck, Dillon. I need more. Oh, please." She arched off the bed, her hips rolling and pressing down to bring me back in. She was just as desperate as I was.

"This is going to be quick. I can't hold back anymore." I gathered her hips in my hands to try and still her. I had no willpower left, and the only thing stopping me from ramming her through the wall was the fact that I didn't want to hurt her. I was a big boy, and even though I could feel her body was more than just wet and ready for me, I didn't know if she was ready for all of me.

"Give it to me, Dillon. I can take it."

That's my girl.

The thought made me smile. I was right. She was my girl. Finally.

I pushed back in and let desire and need take over. I pounded into Keeley relentlessly, only pausing briefly every once in a while to watch her legs shake with her powerful orgasms.

I could feel my release building up inside of me as I pounded into her harder, grunting. My legs tensed and lightning shot through the fibers in my muscles.

"Oh, oh, Dillon!" She screamed my name one more time, and I could feel one deep long tight contraction of her pussy.

"Thank fuck!" I growled as I pumped everything I had into her. My midsection bowed powerfully with every pulse that shot out of me. I had to grab onto the headboard to keep me upright; it felt as if I wouldn't ever stop cumming.

Finally, when every last drop of energy was pulled from my body, I pulled out of her.

She winced as we parted ways.

"Did I hurt you?" I asked I had been rough with her. Usually, I didn't care. As long as the girl wasn't screaming stop, no more, I would keep on going. But with Keeley, I wanted to attempt at least to cherish her.

"Only in a good way." She smiled at me; she was bright-eyed and flushed.

She'd won and I was sure she was gloating in her head. I was grateful that I didn't have to hear it.

Suddenly my peace of mind went straight out the window.

We didn't use a condom.

It was the first time in my life that I had gone raw with anyone. I didn't know what she was thinking about not using a condom.

"Princess, you know I meant everything I said about not letting you go, right?"

She scrunched her eyebrows and sat up to look at me, the cover falling away from her plump breast.

I looked down, and whatever I had wanted to say flew straight out of my mind. I wanted her again.

"Dillon?"

Focus!

RAE B. LAKE

"Uh, yeah, I was just making sure that you knew that I was serious about staying with you."

"Yeah, why are you saying it again?"

I grabbed her around the waist and pulled her to me. I didn't want her to freak out when she realized. "Well, we didn't use a condom, and as much as I left in there, you could for sure be pregnant."

She laughed softly. "No, I couldn't. I have an IUD."

A what and the where?

"Um, ok."

"You have no idea what that is, do you?" She raised her eyebrow at me.

"Not in the least."

"It is a little device implanted into my uterus that stops me from getting pregnant."

Disgust must have been all over my face. That didn't seem safe at all.

She laughed a bit. "No worries. I'm not thinking about getting pregnant at all. But is this a common occurrence for you?"

Thank God! Even though I thought I would step up if she did get pregnant, I never want any kids. Ever.

"No. You're the only woman I have ever fucked without a rubber." I pulled her closer to me. "I'm glad I waited. That shit felt amazing."

"Tell me about it. You're my first without a condom as well, so I think we're all good."

With that out of the way, I pulled her under me again and dove deep into her sweet spot. I didn't think I would ever get enough of her.

CHAPTER 17

Wire

A muffled scream rang out through the room. I smiled and put more effort into getting deeper. I grabbed Keeley's hips, slamming in and out of her tight pussy. I kept waiting to get tired of being with her, for her body to bore me, but it never happened. Every day she would do something else that would drive me wild. It was the little things.

Earlier she had been trying to cook us dinner, and just the motion of her reaching up for a spice jar, her shorts riding up, pulling tight on her ass had me salivating. I had picked her up right then and hauled her over my shoulder, heading straight for bed, which we'd yet to leave.

I pulled her back to me. She was trying to crawl away. It was only natural. I was a big boy and penetrated deep when I had her in doggy style.

"Oh, Dillon. You're so big, soo big… mmm don't stop. Jesus, don't stop." She let her front fall down to the bed, her face in the pillow where she could curse and scream as much as she wanted to.

"That's right, Princess. Take all of me." I tried everything I could to slow down. I knew that if I kept up the same pace, she'd be too sore later on, and we wouldn't be able to have sex again today. That'd be torturous.

I could feel my toes curling, pinpricks colliding on my skin. I was so close to cumming; it was all I could think about. I knew Keeley had cum at least four times, and she was spent, waiting for me to finish. I grabbed her by her hair, yanking her back up toward me so that I was going in from a different angle. The sudden change had me shivering with pleasure. Her wails got higher and longer, her nails digging into my skin.

"Come for me, now. Don't you dare hold back on me." I picked up the pace, but held back in my thrusts to give her a different sensation. I was chasing my release, and I could feel the vibrations coursing through my body as it reared up to explode.

Suddenly she inhaled deeply, her legs shook, her body tensed, her sweet spot pulsed and pulled me in hard.

I threw my head back in ecstasy as I emptied my seed into her, the pulsation of her orgasm enough to keep me coming until she was finished. Finally, she let a rush of air out and moaned low, she pulled her knees up towards her chest, laying right back on the bed in the same position that she had been in previously.

"Babe, you good?" I asked I knew that she was, but my ego could always use a bit more boosting.

"God, yes," she mumbled in her blissed-out state. She snuggled closer into the pillow. I could have counted on one hand the seconds it took her to knock out. She was asleep before I could even slide out of her. Mission accomplished.

I grabbed a cloth out of the linen closet for her and one for me. I cleaned myself off and wet her cloth, washing gently between her legs. She moaned sweetly in her sleep while I took care of her. I tossed the washcloth on the floor, lying down next to her. This was the life, the life that I never knew that I wanted.

This time when I woke up, Keeley was sitting up, on the side of the bed, looking down at something. I crawled up behind her to see what she was doing. There in her hand was my piece. She had the clip out and the bullet out of the chamber.

"What are you doing, Keeley? That isn't a toy." I reached around her and tried to take the gun out of her hand.

She turned towards me with the gun still in her hand and expertly inserted the clip and the extra shell without even batting an eyelash. She handed it back to me after putting the safety on and turned away.

What the hell was that?

There was no way that she learned to do that from a TV show or something. Someone had taught her how to use a gun. If I didn't know any better, I would think that she was a pro.

"You going to tell me where you learned to do that?"

"Good ol' daddy."

"Really?"

"Yup." She sighed and turned away. "I never thought I would want to be with someone who was in this life, but here I am laid up with you."

Was that a jab? "What do you mean someone like me?"

"A killer."

"I do what I have to do." I could feel the tension begin to rise in me. *Was I suddenly not good enough for her?*

She must have noticed my tension because she grabbed my face and turned it towards her. "I know Dillon, and I am not saying that. I understand that you're different. But, growing up with my father and his goons. It made me feel like all of you guys were the same. I was so tired of seeing blood and celebrating when people died. I hate it."

"You were there?"

"Yeah, he would take me along with him when he'd kill, when he would take the lives of those that crossed him. He thought he was teaching me how to be ruthless when all he was teaching me was how to hate him."

"I am sure he was just doing what he thought he needed to do to protect you."

"Oh, he was, but it was just the wrong thing."

"The Diablo crew taught me the same thing. They taught me how to kill, when you kill, and what to kill with. I wouldn't be here if it weren't for them."

"Tell me what you did before them?" She crawled up.

I thought back on my life with my parents, and it was nothing good, just beating after beating, pain after more pain.

"I existed," I said, looking up at the ceiling. "There was never any love in my house, just pain, hunger and hopelessness. I stayed in my little corner at nights, praying that they would die and that I could run away and every morning that I would wake up and they were still alive, I would die a little inside." I looked down at her as I told her the rest of my story. "I am the way that I am because of my father. He would beat me until I broke, until I whimpered and begged for him to stop. Until I told him no more. So, I learned how to turn off my feelings, to turn off my body to everything coming in at me, to take solace in the chaos around me."

"You can't live like that."

"I was doing ok until you showed up." I pulled her tighter to my chest, she felt good there.

"You thought you were," she retorted.

"Yeah, well, I guess I was wrong."

"Tell me about it." She rolled her eyes and poked me in the side.

"Woman, what are you doing to me?"

"The same things you are doing to me."

Was it possible? Did she feel as strongly about me as I did about her? The way that I was feeling right now, it didn't seem possible, but I could hope.

CHAPTER 18

Wire

I walked into the club with my head held high and a big ass smile on my face. I didn't care what anyone said; I was walking on cloud nine.

"What the fuck is that goofy-ass look on your face?"

"Don't be a hater, Clean. It doesn't look good on you."

His eyebrows raised to his hairline. "Oh, yeah, me a hater? That's basically my job description. But you, you're supposed to be the dark brooding type. Now you're sitting here looking like the cat who ate the fucking canary. Why you so fucking happy? Let me guess you finally tried some blow? It's a life-changer, ain't it?"

"No, you fuck. Ain't no one doing anybody's drugs." I rolled my eyes and let the smile slide off my face.

"Yes, he is. But it ain't blow. His drug of choice goes by the name of Keeley," Larry said from behind me.

"Shut the fuck up," I said, trying to be angry about it. I couldn't. He was right.

"Oh boy, your nose is wide the fuck open." Clean looked at me and smiled. He was giving me shit but it did look like he was happy for me.

"Is not," I barely mumbled out.

Liar.

"So, what are you thinking? You gonna patch her? You'll have to talk to Prez if this shit is real."

"Yeah, I am patching her for sure. That's my ol' lady."

For the first time since we'd been friends, Clean jumped up and hugged me. At first, I didn't even know what to do with the sensations in my body. Part of me wanted to push him the fuck off because it was fucking awkward, but he was laughing and clapping me on the back. He was truly happy for me. He was probably the closest thing that I would ever have to a big brother.

"About fucking time! You deserve to be happy my man. I hope she knows what she's getting into." He pulled away, looking me in the eyes.

"I kept telling her to run away. She didn't listen. It's too late for her now."

"I feel you on that." He laughed and we started to walk towards the bar. "So what do you…"

BOOOOM

My ears rang at the sudden loud bang that shook the club walls. Everyone in the building dropped to the deck and covered up.

"What the fuck was that?" Clean screamed when he was able to sit up.

"I don't fucking know!"

I watched as everyone started to run around, getting weapons. Prez and the higher-ups were out of church, already armed and ready to go.

I got up and headed outside with the rest of my brothers, only to see all of their rides had been destroyed.

"What the fuck?" Prez roared as he looked out to the battlefield that was once the parking lot. Every bike, every truck, every car that had been on that side of the compound was now up in flames. The sirens from the fire trucks were getting closer.

"Wire! Take Clean and Gin and see if any of the fuckers are still on the compound." He didn't have to tell me who we were looking for. It was clearly the Tears who had done this. They fucked with my ride; no one messes with my baby and lives.

"You got it, Prez." I made sure that I was carrying and we all took off at a jog to check the perimeter of the clubhouse. I hoped one of them was still around. I wanted to pound someone's face in.

"Can you believe this shit is going down?" Clean huffed out by the side of me. He was never in the best shape.

"Yeah, it was only a matter of time before they brought it to our home."

"Come on guys. Let's go back. Ain't nobody out here," Gin said, clearly anxious to get back into the clubhouse.

Why does he look so scared now? That shit is weird.

"Yeah, he's right. Let's get back inside and see what Prez wants us to do next." Clean stopped running, huffing and puffing, trying to get his breath.

"You're right. We checked the perimeter a few times already. Those fucks are long gone."

We walked, half jogged back to the club. The fire trucks were still outside, handling the small fires from each of the burning vehicles, but the real problems were happening inside. I could hear the uproar before we even made it through the door. They were arguing amongst themselves.

"This is bullshit!"

"Let's go kill those motherfuckers!"

"How are you going to let them get away with this?"

"What the fuck is this shit?"

Everyone was talking at once, trying to be heard over the others. Nothing was being done.

A loud whistle pierced the room, causing everyone to shut the hell up. It was from our treasurer.

"Your President has given you a direct order. There is no conversation, shut the hell up and go about your business." He stared down everyone, daring each of them. What Prez said was law. There should never be any backtalk or questions. Even I knew that.

I walked up to one of the prospects before he could turn and go about his business.

"Prospect!" He stopped in his tracks and turned towards me. "What's the directive? What are we doing?"

He rolled his eyes like he was pissed off. "Lockdown."

What the fuck! No! NO!

A lockdown was something no one wanted, it was an annoyance. The club went into lockdown when there was a threat that we couldn't handle at the time. When we had to get all our ducks in a row or get some out of town help before we made our next move. That meant no one in or out, no biker bunnies, no parties, no drugs, no loud music. Nothing but your room and your thoughts. It was like a fucking prison. Only patched members and the prospects were allowed to be in the club. I looked up as I saw Laura walk into Prez's quarters. His ol' lady was here. Being an ol' lady meant if the enemy couldn't get to your man, they would come after you. All the ol' ladies were already in the building. They were the only women that were allowed.

What about Keeley?

I ran up to Prez before he could make his way up the stairs.

"I have to go out for twenty minutes."

"No boy, I already called a lockdown. You know the rules." He shook his head and tried to continue on his way.

"Fuck the rules! I have to go outside!" I screamed at him. The rest of the higher-ups turned to look at me, some of them with their hands on their pieces. I was about to get my head blown off for talking to Prez like that. "I have to get Keeley. I have to get her."

Prez raised an eyebrow. "She's not patched; she's not allowed."

"Well, patch her, tell me what I have to do?" I asked, starting to feel as if my world was closing in on me.

"You claiming her as your wife?"

Wife?

I hadn't spoken to her about marriage, but short of a big ass ceremony that was exactly what being my ol' lady meant. She was my wife.

"Yes. Yes, she's mine. I need her here." I pleaded with my eyes. I needed her.

He looked over to his men, they weren't going to move. Once lockdown was called, that was it. Whoever was here was here. If you were caught outside, you'd better hide until it was all over.

"I'm sorry, Wire, but we can't do it. We haven't had the ceremony, and no one has vetted her…"

"What the fuck are you talking about?" I roared again, the anger getting the better of me. "I just need twenty fucking minutes! Why are you fucking doing this to me?" I grabbed the nearest chair and I flung it towards the higher-ups, luckily I missed.

Clean was behind me to grab my arms before I could pick anything else up to hurl at the men in front of me.

"Boy, I am going to assume that you have lost your goddamn mind."

"He's just a bit tense, Prez. I got him," Clean said over my head as he wrestled me back from making the biggest mistake I could make.

He got me up the stairs and into my room, but I was fighting him every step of the way. Finally, when he loosened up a bit I was able to break free.

When the hell did Clean get so strong?

I swung on him and he ducked, pushing me away.

"Wire, stop the shit. This is not going to get you anything."

I pulled at my shirt, it was so hot. I felt like the room was choking me. I needed to get out. It was suffocating in the room.

"I need to go outside. I need to go out."

"We can't go out right now, brother. We have to stay inside."

Spots began to pop up in my view and I could feel the sweat begin to pour down my face. I sucked in a breath, but I couldn't get it back out. I pulled on the collar of my shirt again, I needed air.

"I need air. I can't breathe." My eyes darted all over the place looking for an escape, there was none.

"Wire, what's wrong? What is happening to you, man?"

I could hear him, but he sounded so far away.

"Wire!" He had picked up a magazine and was fanning my face, the air felt nice. I closed my eyes and let him continue.

Suddenly, I felt something cold against my neck. I don't even know when he moved, but he'd managed to get a cloth with cold water on my neck to cool me down.

"Take some deep breaths in and out."

I did what he asked, and after a while I was able to breathe normally.

"Well, that looked like it sucked."

"It felt worse than it looked, I promise you." I felt like such a pansy. I am supposed to be the pain enforcer, and here I was whimpering like a little bitch.

"It's cool. It's over now. You need some water or something?"

I looked up at Clean, and I saw no pity in his eyes, just concern. I knew he would keep my secret. I made a mental note to thank him for it at a later date.

"Yeah, there should be some in the mini-fridge."

"Mini-fridge?" He looked at me like I had wounded him, "When the fuck did you get a mini-fridge? You selfish bastard!"

He stalked off towards the corner, all the while muttering profanities about how I don't like to share and how he would never keep food away from me. Before I knew it, he had everything that I was stashing away out and opened to eat.

CHAPTER 19

Wire

It had been over a week since we were able to leave the clubhouse, and everyone was getting antsy. The rest of the club were already chomping at the bit, pretty much begging Prez to let them out. Of course, he didn't. The higher-ups were sure from the rumors that the Tears had gotten a few other crews to rise up against us. We were about to be outnumbered and outgunned fast.

"Wire, what are you doing?" Clean knocked on my door. He was bored, as usual.

"Go away!" I lay in the bed, punching my pillow. I hadn't gotten a good night's sleep since the last night that I was with Keeley.

"No, come on, bro. Play street fighters with me!" For a grown-ass man, he sure liked his video games.

"No!"

I saw the flashing lights of my phone and reached over to see my angel's face.

"Keeley," I growled. I was missing her more than I thought I would. I'd been speaking to her every day, making sure that she stayed safe. I even made her carry a blade with her every time she decided that she needed to go out. Still, it wasn't enough. I wanted her to be with me so I could keep her safe.

"Yes, lover, how are you?"

"Fine," I said rather curtly.

"You not sleeping good, huh?"

We hadn't been together for that long, but she already knew most of my moods. I was a real jerk when I didn't get my rest.

"No," I mumbled into the phone

"I'm sorry, babe. If it makes you feel any better, I am missing you too."

"Yeah?"

"Yeah, so much."

"How much?" I could hear her breathing heavily over the phone. If I didn't know any better I would think that she was playing with herself.

"Enough that I am always soaking wet for you. I am so ready for you, Dillon." She moaned into the phone softly, "I need you."

Fuck, she's going to end me!

"Keeley, what are you doing?" I could feel myself growing harder with every passing second, every moan from her lips.

"I wish you were here. I wish you were deep inside of me." Her breath was coming faster now.

I groaned as I palmed my erection through my pants. I wasn't going to make this lockdown. She was driving me absolutely crazy. We'd been going at each other nonstop before the lock-down, and to just stop cold turkey was enough to make me sell my soul, just to feel her under me one more time.

"Oh, Dillon." A low moan filtered through the phone.

"Don't you fucking do it, don't cum."

"Oh Dillon, I need to, I have to."

I could hear her taking in deep breaths, trying to calm herself down.

"Don't, I want all of it. The next time I am in you, I want juices to run down your legs. I want it all." I gripped my still covered manhood. I was about to have some serious blue balls.

"Please, Dillon." She mewled through the phone at me.

"Nope, I want it all."

"Ugh, you are so mean to me."

I laughed, I could practically see her pouting through the phone.

"No, Princess. I am going to be mean to you the next time I see you though, and you won't be able to walk straight for at least a day."

"Promises. Promises." She chuckled lightly through the phone.

"Well, I have to go but be on the lookout for your own form of torture."

With that, she hung up the phone.

What the hell does that mean?

I looked at the phone like it was going to tell me the meaning of life, it gave me no answers.

I turned over in my bed, taking care not to crush my already engorged member.

I punched the pillows again. There was no way I was getting any sleep now. I was about to get up and find Clean to see if he still wanted to go a round or two in Street Fighters, but then my phone beeped a few times, indicating I had a new message.

I grabbed up my phone again and saw that the messages were from Keeley. She was sending me photos. I immediately shot up in the bed. She had on dark green lingerie, the top barely covered her large breasts and her nipples were clearly hard and pebbled. The next photo was of her pulling down one of the cups so that she'd be able to get to one of her breasts, so she could squeeze it. The next photo was of her hand trailing down her stomach toward her mound. In the next photo, she was bottomless, and her hand was buried deep.

A text message popped up next. "Don't worry. I'm saving it all for you. But you need some sleep. I hope these help."

I tore my clothes off as I ran for my shower. I had to release this tension and with those photos of Keeley floating around in my head I was not about to have any problems.

"Wire, get your ass in here boy," Prez called up from downstairs.

"On my way." I hopped out of my bed. I'd had some of the best sleep that I'd had in a long while after Keeley's gifts.

I walked towards Prez, waiting to see what kind of page we were going to be on. If he was pissed or if he understood. Either way, I wasn't going to apologize. *Fuck that.*

He stared me down for a second. "You speak to your woman?"

"Yea, she's good, Prez. Staying safe."

"That's good to hear, son." He gave a small smile. I guess he understood my anger. "Come on." He turned and started walking towards the church. I followed but stopped before I could get to the door. Only the higher-ups were allowed in church, it wasn't my place to go in.

"What you waiting on boy, let's go." He held the door open for me.

"Ok." *Why do they want me in there?* I didn't understand. I walked in and stood right by the door, in case one of the other higher-ups decided that I had overstepped my bounds.

"Wire, if you don't stop acting like a scared puppy…sit your ass down."

What? They want me at the table? What the hell is this?

I sat down where Prez pointed, waiting on eggshells for someone to tell me what was going on.

"I won't sugar coat it. We're at a bad place right now, and we need to be at one hundred percent. We are missing a big piece of our court. We have no VP. We think that should be you."

I blinked a few times. I just couldn't understand what they were talking about. I was just a lowly pain manager. *They wanted me?*

"What are you talking about? What about Gin? He's been here way longer than I have."

"That's true, but something has been off with Gin for a while now. We don't think that he is up to something like this." Prez leaned forward in the chair. "What? You don't want the job?"

"Of course, I want the job. I just didn't think you guys would ever think of me."

"We aren't blind. We see how dedicated you are to the club, Wire. We always thought that you had a death wish. I think this little woman of yours might have just changed that up, and I look forward to meeting her," Mick, one of the founding members, said.

"I am sure she will be happy to meet you all, as well." I settled a little more into the chair. "So, what does this mean exactly? Am I VP or is there a trial period?"

"For sure, a trial period. Work with us to get out of this shit and find out how it started, and then the job is yours."

"Ok, so where are we at right now?"

"Right to business. I like it."

With that, they filled me in on everything that was going down, how the Tears had already recruited three other crews to come after us, but they weren't loyal. If anything really serious were to go down, they would leave the Tears in an instant. You can't really expect mercenaries to be any different. They told me that Monte still had a hard on for me. He was telling everyone that I wasn't to be killed, he wanted to do it himself.

I was pleased to find out that we did have a few other chapters of Wings coming to help us out. We had other chapters around the nation, and we only called on them when we needed them, and we needed them now.

We'd been getting ready for a war for some time now, but all of a sudden, it seemed as if all the pieces were in place, just waiting for the other one to strike.

Just waiting.

CHAPTER 20

<u>Keeley</u>

"Babe, I'm almost done. As soon as I put this last specimen in, I will pack up and be on my way," I said sweetly into the phone. Dillon was always so worried about me. Honestly, after the well ordeal, I hadn't even seen anyone from Chaos. He wasn't going to take any chances though. It was super cute but getting a bit annoying. I wasn't used to having to tell anyone my every move.

"So, stay on the phone until you are out."

"Dillon," I said, trying to let him hear my annoyance.

"Fine, just call me when you are on your way home. Cool?"

"Yes, lover. I'm almost done. Ok? Like twenty minutes."

"Yeah, later."

"Bye babe."

I clicked off my phone and shoved it in my pocket so I could put on my static-free gear and get this done.

I was almost finished, humming a little song when the lights suddenly went out.

"Gosh darn generator."

The staff was always forgetting to fill the generator with fuel. So at least once a week or so we would have a blackout. Then one of us would have to run down and turn it back on before we compromised any of the specimens.

I walked out of the lab, taking my lab suit off and slowly making my way towards the pump downstairs. It took me all of five minutes to get there. I could find the supplies I needed in the dark; I'd done this so many times. I reached down to get the fuel we already had it in pre-packaged jugs. I walked over to the fuel tank and opened the top…

Shit, someone cut the line.

This wasn't the usual blackout. Someone cut the line so that the lights would go out. I dropped the fuel immediately and fumbled in my back pocket to call Wire. Someone was in here with me, and no one would come looking for me for some time. This was bad.

I finally managed to get it out of my pocket and started to look for his number so I could dial when a hand grabbed my wrist, twisting it so the phone would fall to the ground.

"Hello there, girly."

I'd heard that voice before. It was one of the same ones from the woods that day. They'd come to finish the job.

I screamed in pain. He had my hand at an awkward angle with tons of pressure. If he pushed any more, it would break. "Get the hell off me!" I yelled at him like it would do any good.

"Ah, I'm sorry, but I really can't do that." He stepped in a bit closer to me, his sour breath caressing the rim of my ear, made me want to puke. "There's something that we need you to do. Something very simple, in fact." He stepped back, and even in the darkness, I could see the cold crazy in his eyes.

"I need you to call, Wire. Get him out of his club and to come to you."

"What, I can't, they're on lockdown. He can't come out."

He twisted my hand a little more, causing a fresh wave of pain to go cascading through my body.

"Oh, I think you can. You haven't even tried," he said.

"No, I won't do it."

"No?" It sounded like he was unbelieving, that he thought I was somehow playing around with him. I had something for his ass.

I waited for him to get close enough to my face, and with all the force I could muster, I raised my knee into his groin, hard enough that I could have sworn I heard a pop.

I took off as fast as I could in the opposite direction. There were so many different ways out of the complex, and I knew each and every one.

"Fuck!" He roared from behind me. I assumed he was still holding his junk on the floor, but I wasn't going to turn around and find out. "She's getting away!"

I kept my eyes on the tunnel ahead of me. There were other people in the building, and I could hear the footfalls in the background as they came looking for me.

I wished I'd just listened to Dillon and stayed on the phone; he would've known what to do. He would have helped me.

I turned towards the offices on the first floor. I didn't know if they were out by the front, but I could use the windows in the office to crawl out, maybe towards the back, and keep running.

I made it to the back rooms and could see the night light beaming in through the window. It only took me a quick second to open it and slip one leg out. I turned my head towards the inside of the complex. I couldn't hear the footfalls anymore. Maybe they'd gone the wrong way in the complex. It was easy to get lost in here, and I was glad that the complexity of the building might have just saved my life.

I jumped out of the first-floor window, feeling the cool air blast against my face. It took me no time at all to run to my truck. I needed to get out of there. I reached into the glove compartment and took out my keys, jamming them into the ignition.

"Where do you think you're going?"

I screamed loud and high as I looked in the rearview mirror and saw someone sitting in my back seat. I tried to get out of the car but the person grabbed my hair and slammed me hard against the steering wheel. I fought to stay conscious, but I could feel the blackness winning the battle.

"You should have just called him, and now things are going to get worse for you. I was really hoping not to have to mess up that pretty body of yours." He pulled me out of the front seat and into the passenger. I couldn't even fight back. I was so weak.

"I hope he loves you enough to come for you. That's all we want."

I grunted at him, unable to make coherent sentences anymore. I felt the car jerk and pull out and the back doors open as other people got in. Then we were off, and I was about to have a fucked up night.

CHAPTER 21

Wire

I'd gotten no sleep. Keeley hadn't called me like she said she would and I was worried. That was why I didn't do this girlfriend, shit. I bet her ass fell asleep, watching some bullshit movie while I was over here, worrying my ass off. I sat in the corner, dialing and re-dialing her phone number but it just kept going to voicemail.

There was a loud knock on the club door. It was so quiet that the sound echoed off the whole complex.

It was almost four am, so whoever was at the door wasn't bringing good news. I walked out of my room, seeing Clean come out of his, wiping sleep out of his eye. Prez and a few other higher-ups who had been sitting at the bar walked up as well. Larry, who was on watch, went up to the door to see who it was.

"What do you want?" He called out before he even opened the door. His piece ready to fire in his hand.

A squeaky female voice shouted back through the door. "Some guys paid me some money to bring this here."

Larry opened the door slowly to see a little girl, dirty and small, holding out a little brown envelope. She obviously wasn't a threat but he didn't put his gun away. You never knew what could go down.

Her trembling hand continued to hold out the envelope as Prez walked up and took it from her. "Larry, give her some change."

"For fucking what?"

Prez only had to look at him before he dug in his pocket and gave the small child a fifty, which she happily took and skipped away.

Prez opened up the envelope slowly in case something decided to

138

pop out but there was nothing that I could see. Clean was standing near him, as well as Larry. Their eyes darted to whatever was in the envelope.

"Oh Shit," Clean said under his breath before his eyes jumped up to me.

What the fuck is he looking at me for?

I took a step towards Prez, itching to see what was in the envelope now. From the way they were all looking at it and then at me, I could tell I had something to do with it. *What was it?*

Clean took a few steps forward, blocking my path.

"Chill out, brother." He put a hand on my shoulder.

Is this fucking sympathy?

"What's in the envelope?" I asked quietly, needing to know what it was, but part of me was a little scared to find out.

"Nothing you need to worry about right now."

I looked over his shoulder to Prez, who was now going through what looked to be a few photos, and every once in a while, he would look back up to me. A small twinge of fear in his eyes.

"Fuck that! What's in the pictures!" I tried to push past Clean but he caught hold of my arms, holding me back. Larry was the next one to jump in and help him.

"We'll figure it out. Don't worry. Don't worry." Clean bearhugged me, not wanting to hurt me but not wanting me to get away.

What the fuck was in the pictures?

I couldn't see it but there was only one reason to shield me away from them, only one person.

"Let him go," Prez called out as he put the photos back into the envelope and began to walk toward church.

I followed him as quickly as possible.

"Prez, what's in the pictures?" I asked before we even got into church properly.

"Take a seat Wire."

"No, I don't want a fucking seat. I want to know what you saw!"

I was fighting against my anger. I was trying so hard to push it back down. I knew whatever was going on wasn't Prez's fault, but I was too on edge.

He locked the door and pulled up the photos. "We can't react Wire. That's what they want. Our allies will be here in a few days, and we will handle this, but we can't give in."

I had blocked out whatever he was talking about; my focus was on the photos in front of me.

Keeley.

They had her tied up and naked in a chair, and blood was pouring down her face and chest. The next photo was of her tied down to a table with a wet rag over her face, her legs kicked up. They were waterboarding her. Finally, the last picture was of her in the corner, crying with cuts on her body, and rats surrounding her. They'd set rats on her. My legs buckled as I tried to take in what I was looking at. Rats were going to eat the woman I loved, and he wanted me to wait? Yeah, he was out of his mind. I felt my muscles go numb as I looked back up to him. Prez was still talking, clearly trying to calm me down. I didn't hear a word. I simply turned, opened the door and walked up to my room. That's where all my tools were. I would need a fucking arsenal for what I had planned for these fucks.

I gathered everything that I could carry. The barbed wire, the knives, the guns, blow torch, you know the necessities. I put them in a duffel bag and a backpack, and walked out of the room to see all the higher-ups and the rest of the club up and out waiting for me.

Clean met me before I could make my way to the bottom of the stairs.

"Brother, we are on lockdown. We can't go right now."

"Move."

He backed up a bit, and let me continue on my path. Everyone knew not to mess with me when I was like this, numb to the world. I was pretty sure you could shoot me right in the face and I would still keep coming.

"Wire, where the fuck do you think you're going?" Mick called out as I made my way past everyone, not even hearing what any of them were trying to say. "If you walk out that door, that's it for you. Consider that your trial period over!"

I stopped and dropped what I had. "Did you just fucking threaten me?" I snarled at him. I couldn't believe the audacity.

"I'm not scared of you!" He said back, but the small tremble in his throat told me otherwise.

"Wire, we know what you are going through-" Prez started to say.

"Bullshit!" I roared. "You don't know shit about what I'm going through right now. Your woman is in the back safe in your bed, while mine is with our enemy being fucking tortured and you think I give a shit about a seat at the table or this fucking club right now? Take my fucking kutte! Disband me, do what the fuck you got to do. But I promise you, I am walking the fuck out of this club and I am going to get my woman. You can all sit here on your asses if you want. Me, I got fucking business to handle." I stared everyone who would meet my eyes, down. I dared them to say something else. I grabbed my shit and walked out of the building, and no one else tried to stop me.

It was only ten am but I had already found, six of the Tears of Chaos brothers. There were six fewer members now. I drove up to another hideout that I had on my list of places that they liked to be. I found two more there, and one of them was none other than the notorious Scotty. He was fully patched now. *Good for him.*

I walked in and everyone that wasn't a Tear took off in the opposite direction. I was covered in blood and guts. I didn't care. I needed to know where Keeley was and nothing was going to stop me. I grabbed both of them by the neck and dragged them to the back. Locking the door and handcuffing them to poles in the walls, looked like steam pipes, nice and sturdy. They wouldn't break free for a long time.

Scotty was screaming; at least I thought he was. I'd been in a numb state for hours. He was gagged as he watched me torture his club mate. He didn't give me the information that I wanted, so I removed the skin off his face with a paring knife. It was a slow process, and he was unconscious before I'd finished, but I wanted to make sure that I had completed the job. I slit his throat when I was done, just for good measure.

Finally, I moved on to Scotty. "Where are they keeping Keeley?" I turned on the blow torch and then pulled the gag out of his mouth.

"She's down by the pier," he blurted out as soon as his mouth was able to work properly. I am pretty sure he bit his tongue, trying to get the words out. There was nothing like a cooperative mark. He already knew what I could do, and he obviously didn't want to feel the pain I could dole out again.

"By the pier, where?" I put the blow torch down near him, not close enough to touch him but close enough that he could still feel the heat.

"Ah, I don't know," he stuttered.

I picked up the blow torch and quickly swiped it down his midsection watching as the skin bubbled angrily. He screamed and squealed, pulling at the handcuffs, but he couldn't get free.

"I swear on my life, Wire. I don't know exactly where. It has to be at the lower end, where they bring in the fish and crabs. There is a big warehouse right where they are keeping for Mermaid Fishery. You should go today. Most of the club is out at a meeting, and they won't be back for a long while. She'll be mostly alone. Maybe only a few guards." He looked up at me, pleading with his eyes that this was enough information to get me to leave him alone. It was.

I grabbed the hair at the back of his head and brought the flame close to his face.

"If I get there and you're wrong, I'm going to come for you, and your dick won't be the only thing that I will cut off. I hope you value your life, and that of your family."

I saw him suck in a huge breath, mention a family to a mark, and they were usually willing to do anything that you ask of them.

He nodded his head, a quick tear falling down his face. He had pissed himself and I was ready to get out of there, I hit him with the butt of my gun until he fell unconscious. I had to get my woman.

CHAPTER 22

Wire

I walked into my club. I needed more weapons if I was going to the holding spot. Scotty said it was going to be with minimal guards, but I wasn't about to walk in there without any protection.

"Wire! Stop, dammit." Clean stood right in front of me. It was the only way I could hear that he was talking to me. The words were sort of muted. I'd had to really focus to see that he was talking to me.

"I got shit to do, Clean. Move."

"We're trying to help you, brother."

That caught my attention. *What did he mean, help me?* If that was code for keeping me locked up until they thought it was a good time to go after them, then I was going to have to punch him right in the face and move on.

"What are you talking about?"

"Prez held a meeting after you left. He agreed with you. He's lifting the lockdown so we can get Keeley. I've been looking for you all morning."

They were going to help me? Not kick me out?

"Really?"

"Yeah, brother and none of the guys were going to speak out against the Prez and the new V.P." He shot me a wink and lightly punched me in the arm.

Apparently, the word was out that I was up for VP.

"I'm not VP yet, and from what was said earlier, I don't think I passed my trial."

"Shit, you were calm for someone who just found out their woman was tied up in the enemy's basement. No one would have acted any differently. All the other brothers want no one but you."

When did I get so high up on everyone's list?

"Well, I'm about to end it now. I know where Keeley is. I only came back here to get some more heat."

"Ok, hold up. I know Larry, the prospects and a few others are here. Let us get our gear." He backed away from me, making sure that I wasn't going to leave without him.

"You got three minutes and then I'm out." I turned from him and made my way up the stairs.

I grabbed everything I could carry that was in the form of a gun and all the ammo that I could ever need. It took me all of two minutes. Loaded with three semi-automatic weapons, a sawed-off shotgun and a fully automatic Uzi. I walked out to see Larry, Clean, Prez, the prospects, Ryder and Archer, and all of them were fully decked out. Clean even had a few grenades strapped to his hip. They weren't playing games. My brothers were ready to go to war for me.

"Where is the little lady?" Prez asked.

"She's supposedly by the pier near the Mermaid Fishery warehouse. He couldn't tell me the exact location only that it's very close to that. He also said that now would be a great time to get her since she'll be pretty much alone for the day. Shouldn't be too many people shooting at us."

"Do you believe the source?" Archer asked.

"Yeah, it was Scotty. He was determined not to feel my wrath again."

Everyone nodded.

"Alright, we go in quick and quiet. Luckily there are only three places near that end of the pier that she can be in," Prez said, taking lead of the situation immediately.

"You got it, boss."

"Let's go get your woman." Prez clapped me on the back and we made our way to the trucks.

We went by the three buildings that were in the area and the first two were duds, nothing there but equipment and seagulls. The last building that we went to seemed like it was the winner. There were two guards outside, their Tears of Chaos patches easily visible.

"Clean, you, Wire and Archer go through the front, and the rest of us will find a way to go through the back. If you can't get in clean, hold back until we get in and we will take out these two," Prez said.

I watched as they ran off around the corner.

"Archer, can you take the one on the left out?" We called him Archer because he was the best shot in the whole club, he was a sniper at one time in a past life.

I watched as he set up his rifle, took a deep breath, and as he gently exhaled, took out the man to the left, a single shot in the center of his head. I bet the dumbass didn't realize when he woke up this morning that guarding that girl would be the last thing he'd do.

As soon as the guard dropped, the other guard opened fire in the direction that we were in. He was shooting far left from where we were, but one lucky bullet hit a machine, ricocheting and striking Clean right in the arm.

"Fuck!" He yelled as the blood began to seep down his shirt.

"Goddammit!" I ran over to him and put pressure on the wound. Clean was the last one that I wanted hurt right now. He always had my back.

"Wire, get out of here. He isn't guarding the door. That is your way in."

"Nah, I have to get you out of here first."

"Wire go! I got him!" Archer said over the spray of bullets as the lonely guard finally figured out where we were. Archer looked up once and fired. He was right on the mark as usual. With the last guard down, I ran into the building, looking to see if I could see her. There was nothing around but fishing equipment and abandoned cars.

Prez, Max and the others moved into the building from the back. "I didn't see anyone when we came in. I think the two at the front were the only ones here. Scotty was telling the truth."

"He better pray he was." I jogged down toward the stairs, from the pictures she was in a basement of sorts.

I took off at a sprint, not even waiting for any backup. Keeley was close; she had to be.

I opened one of the doors, and there was nothing in there but an overturned bed, some rats and a bucket. I was about to close the door when I saw something flesh-colored in the corner behind the bed. I walked up slowly and when I noticed it was a pair of dainty feet, all the breath left my body.

"Is that her?" I heard Prez ask from behind me, but my eyes were fixated on the unmoving feet lying on the floor. She had to be ok; I couldn't be too late.

"Keeley?" I said as I continued my slow stalk toward her body. She didn't answer. Finally, I got to the bed and pushed it away from her. She was pale and curled into a ball, some cloth rolled up and wrapped around her body. She was trying to keep away the rats.

I shook my head in disgust, how had I let this happen to her.

I knelt down behind her and reached under to pick her up.

"No. Don't you fucking touch me. Don't touch me."

She woke from her slumber, a fresh set of tears streaming down from her still closed eyes. She swung her fists blindly, hitting me in the face and shoulder. I could have cried from relief; she was still here with me, still alive.

"Babe, it's me." She was still swinging. I cleared my throat and spoke again, "Keeley, open your eyes, baby, it's me."

She opened her eyes slowly, one was slightly swollen and blood-shot, so I wasn't sure if she could see me clearly. I rubbed my hand along her face.

"Dillon?"

"Yes, Princess. I'm here."

She reached up around my neck and squeezed with everything she had, kissing the side of my face and my eyes, everywhere she could reach. More tears were streaming down her battered face, but this time, she was smiling.

"Oh my god, I didn't think you would find me. I didn't think I'd-"

I cut her off with a soft kiss on the lips.

"Nothing would keep me from you, Keeley. You're mine."

"Yes. I am yours."

Finally, with my girl in my arms, I walked out of there, feeling just a bit lighter and at peace.

CHAPTER

Wire

Keeley was put directly into intensive care when we got her to the hospital. Those bastards beat her, waterboarded her, and stuck her in a room with rats who were eating off little chunks of her at a time. The doctors were all worried about the infections that any of them could have transferred to her. They were also concerned about the condition of her lungs. She'd pneumonia from the water she'd inhaled. They'd had to place a breathing tube in her throat along with a feeding tube in her nose to get some nutrients into her.

Prez put the club back in lockdown, but he and the rest of the brothers knew that there was no way that I was going to leave Keeley. They would need to pry my dead fingers from her bed if they were going to get me to leave. What would get me to leave was Keeley.

The longer I stayed, the more I couldn't see how she'd want to be with me. I had caused so much grief in her life. I had taken her sweet, calm life and inserted all my bullshit. There was no way for me to make it up to her. None.

I watched her sleep, wanting to be there every time she woke up.

Her eyes fluttered open and her face immediately fell into a frown around the tube in her throat.

That was all the confirmation that I needed.

"Keeley, you have every reason to hate me. I've done nothing but destroy your life. I am so sorry. I just wanted to make sure that you were going to be ok. I'll leave you be."

She reached up to the tube that was in her mouth and tried to pull it out. I grabbed her hand just before she could.

"Are you crazy? What the hell are you thinking? This shit is keeping you alive!"

She glared at me and dug her nails into the skin on my hand, causing me to hiss and pull my hand away in pain. She grabbed at the tube again and began to yank, gagging as the thick tube began to come up. It was quicker than I thought it was going to be. She gagged a few times.

I walked to the door ready to leave and get a nurse.

"Always running," her voice rasped.

"What?" I turned back to see what she was talking about.

"Always fucking running away." This time it was clearer.

"Fuck that! I don't run from anything. I don't belong with you, Keeley. I told you before that my life wasn't for you. And here you are for a second time in the damn hospital because of me."

The nurses heard the commotion and made their way into the room, "Miss you can't have that out yet," one of the nurses reprimanded her, while the other went to go fetch the doctor so they could put it back in.

"Really, because of you? I didn't know you were the one who was chasing me through the lab, or the one who tied me up, or the one who beat me. Tell me which one of those people were you again? Because I'm not sure."

I rolled my eyes at her, of course, she had something to say.

"No, of course, I didn't personally do any of those things, but can you honestly say that you would have had any of those things happen to you if I hadn't been in your life?"

"No, but I also can't say that anyone would've been around to save me from those people."

I shook my head; she was missing the whole point. "Keeley, I wouldn't have had to save you-"

"I love you, Dillon," she looked at me, expectant.

My brain had stopped working. No one had ever told me they loved me. At least nobody of consequence. I had had a few women scream it when I was fucking them, but I never paid any mind to that. It didn't make me throw them out any slower. But to hear it from Keeley, even after everything I had put her through? I was in awe.

"You love me?"

"Of course, I do, Dillon. You're worthy of love. Don't you see that?" She reached a hand to me, and I walked over to her, placing my hand in hers.

"Do you love me too?" She asked.

"I think I do. I don't know. I don't know what it feels like to love someone."

"Well, tell me what you feel."

"I feel like if you were to go, I would die. I want to see you every day. I want you to be happy more than I want my next breath. I feel like my life is complete when you hold me. All I think of is you; you're my everything."

A tear rolled down her cheek. "Yeah, that's love."

I kissed away her tears and laid down in the bed next to her as close as I could. I needed this woman more than I needed my life. I would never be without her again.

CHAPTER 24

Wire

I stayed by Keeley's side all night long as the nursing staff came and went giving her medication and checking her stats. Luckily the doctor was able to leave the tube out of her throat as long as she promised to keep the oxygen mask on.

I tried to ask her what had happened when she was with the Tears, but every time she opened her mouth to speak, she would cry a bit, causing me to get more and more furious. In the end, we just decided it was best to talk about it some other time.

It was while I was watching her sleep that Prez decided to call me.

I hurried out of the room so that I wouldn't wake her. After everything that she had gone through, she needed all the sleep that she could get.

"Speak," I answered when I was safely away from her door.

"How is that little lady of yours doing?" Prez asked it meant a lot to me that he was concerned for her. It was a testament to his character.

"She's in good spirits, healing up."

"Good, I'm glad to hear it." He let out a deep breath. "We still haven't been able to locate Monte, but word on the street is most of his club has disbanded. They thought he was taking this grudge a bit too far. No one wants to go one on one with you."

"Well, after what they did to her, I wouldn't want to go one on one with me either."

"But we still have a problem. It seems he's still trying to get people together to come after us. It would be a suicide mission, but it seems

151

like he doesn't care as long as he gets to us. And somehow people are being picked off."

"What?" That shouldn't be possible in a lockdown.

"I had to start letting people out, wives were calling, kids crying. So, everyone was going out on their own accord. Six brothers from our allies in New York were taken out by some kind of bomb, and Gin is MIA."

"What the fuck?"

"Yeah, it's getting crazy out there. That's what I wanted to warn you about. I don't think that they will come at you while you're in the hospital. Too many witnesses, but watch your ass when you go out. Be suspicious of everyone."

"For sure, I'm not worried about it."

"Cut the shit! Be worried about it."

"You got it, Prez. I'll be on the lookout."

"Ok, and I am not telling you to take any time away from your woman, but if you happen to run into Gin anywhere tell him to bring his ass in, he's been gone for days and no one knows what's going on with him."

"For sure. If I run into him, I'll tell him."

"Good."

"Prez, did you ever think that maybe…" I stopped my thought, what I was about to say could get me in serious trouble. You never go against one of your brothers, never.

"Speak."

"Nah, it's stupid. I haven't gotten enough sleep. My brain is being paranoid."

"Ah, I think I know where you're going. It passed through my mind too. I pray on everything that we're wrong.

He hung up without any further instruction and I took my ass back to Keeley.

"Hey, I thought you went home," she said, having woken up while I was on the phone outside.

"Nah, just a call I needed to take." I took my seat next to her bed and held her hand. "How are you feeling?"

"Not so great, my back hurts a bit." She shifted in her bed, trying to find a comfortable position.

"Hold still. I'll ring the nurse." I reached over and pressed the call bell several times. It always took them forever to come.

"You look like you need some sleep." She raised her hand and wiped it down my face. I hadn't shaved in days and it looked like it.

"I'm good."

"Yes, ma'am. Did you call?" A nurse was at the door, looking like she was a bit annoyed to be disturbed. If I could get away with it, I would have put her head through the wall.

"Yes, do you think I could get a bit of pain medication? My back is killing me." Keeley tried to adjust herself again.

"Sure, I'll be right in."

I watched as the nurse went to the cart and pulled out a bag of medication to hang on her IV. "You should be feeling better in no time." She set her up and walked out of the room.

I watched as her eyes fluttered a bit. "You got some of the good stuff in there, huh?"

She giggled a bit. "I'm sorry, Dillon. I am such bad company right now."

"Please, I can meditate or some shit, as long as you're feeling better, I can entertain myself."

"You should go home and get some sleep."

"No woman, stop saying it. I'm not going home."

"You're so stubborn."

"Look who's talking."

Suddenly, the same nurse who had just put the pain medication on ran in and snatched the medication away.

"Is something wrong?" Keeley asked.

"Oh, you can't have this medication, I didn't notice they updated your chart this morning."

"Why can't I have it? It's what I was getting yesterday, right?" Keeley was skeptical. I was just beginning to think that this nurse was incompetent.

"It is, but it's no good for someone in your condition."

"My condition?"

The nurse looked from Keeley to me back to Keeley.

"Did anyone come to talk to you yesterday about your bloodwork?"

"No, I assumed everything was fine. Did something turn up?"

The nurse bit her lip. "Yes, but I think maybe we should wait for your doctor."

"What condition?" I asked brusquely. Whatever it was, we would beat it together. Maybe it was cancer, an infection or something.

"Yes, please, just tell me. I will worry about it all day if you make me wait for the doctor. What did the blood tests show?"

She still looked like she wasn't sure if she should tell Keeley. "Just fucking tell us. She has a right to know. If she has other questions, then she can wait for the doctor."

"Fine!" The nurse rolled her eyes at me then settled on Keeley's face, she smiled a bit. "Well, the tests show that you're expecting." She smiled a bit brighter.

"What?" Keeley's face went as pale as the sheet she had covering her.

"You're about two months pregnant."

"That is impossible." Keeley shook her head, clearly not believing what she was being told. "I have an IUD. I can't be pregnant."

"IUDs are only about 99% effective. You are pregnant, for sure. We can get an ultrasound in here later if you would like."

Keeley took a few breaths in. "Yeah, that would be great."

I watched as the nurse left the room.

"Dillon, I don't know how this happened."

I just looked at her, my body had gone numb again. I could hear what she was saying, but it sounded like she was underwater, so far away.

"Dillon, talk to me. We have to talk about this." Her pale face began to flush with color, she was getting upset.

I opened my mouth to say something, but nothing was coming out, the only word that I could hear in my head was *'pregnant'*.

She's pregnant? I just couldn't wrap my head around it. There was no way. *I can't do this. I need to get out.*

I stood up, heard the air woosh past my ears.

"Dillon, what are you doing? Please talk to me." The tears were starting to trail down her face again and there was nothing that I could do to make her feel any better.

I turned towards the door; I had to leave. I had to.

"Dillon, don't you dare leave me now. Not after all this. I need you." Great big tears were falling from her eyes, but I couldn't stop my legs from moving.

CHAPTER 25

Wire

I walked into the clubhouse, my brain still in a fog as to what was going on with my life. I couldn't wrap my head around the fact that she was having a baby. *My baby.* There was no way that she had been with anyone else; I trusted her enough to know that.

But she had told me I didn't need to worry. She told me that pregnancy wasn't a possibility that it was safe, and I believed her, I trusted her.

Never a-fucking-gain!

I was so pissed at her. It felt like she was trying to get rid of me. She was going to leave me now for sure. She was going to have someone else in her life to give all her love to, and now when I just got it, I didn't want to share her love. I wanted it all for myself. Selfish but I didn't care.

How was I supposed to care for a kid? I couldn't. I wasn't even going to attempt to. She would be a single mother because I had no idea what I would be able to offer that kid besides whiskey and profanity.

By the time I had made it to my room, I had no idea if any of my brothers had spoken to me or if any of them were even there. I just wanted this day to end. *Maybe this was all a bad dream.*

I laid down on my bed. I want this day to be over. As I closed my eyes, I let the numbness take over completely. I just wanted to be away from all of this.

Someone outside had other plans. The door to my room rattled with the pounding of someone trying to get in. I didn't even attempt to get up to open the door, and whoever was outside didn't seem to want to wait anyway.

Clean kicked my door in. He broke the entire door off the hinges, literally.

"What the fuck are you doing in bed? You're an absolute pussy!"

I could hear him insulting me, but I couldn't get myself to muster up the strength to defend myself.

"Get the fuck up." He was standing over me, his eyes wild and daring.

"Go away." It was all I could get out.

"Why in all the shit did Keeley call me crying that you ran out on her while she is lying up in the hospital in pain and pregnant."

I tried to roll over and ignore him. "No, you will not run away from this!" He grabbed my leg and dropped me hard on the floor, which got my blood boiling. I jumped up and pushed him away. I swung a right at him and connected to his jaw, but it did nothing to slow him down. He popped my head back twice with two quick jabs followed by an uppercut. His speed caught me off guard. I tried to wrap him up but he was way stronger than me, and he threw me against the wall. I was tired of fighting. I just wanted him to leave me alone.

"What part of get out did you not understand?"

"The part where you think I give a shit about what you had to say. Get your ass back to that hospital and take care of your woman!"

"I can't!" I sat on my bed with my head in my hands. "I can't."

"That's bullshit. Get off your ass and go."

"She's going to leave. I don't want to deal with that shit. I can't be a father. It would never work."

"How the hell would you know?" He sat down on the bed next to me, the fight clearly out of his mind already. "You have to try. Everyone knows you love that woman, she knows it, your enemies know it. Now that she has given you an extension of the both of you to love, you're just going to deny her? Where's the badass that I knew who'd take on any challenge? This is how my new VP acts when shit gets hard?

"You always yell and beat on your VP's? If so I don't know if I want the job," I said, not taking my head out of my hands.

"Come on, Wire. Family comes first. Go back to your woman."

He was right. I knew he was but I just couldn't get myself to do it.

"Alright brother, I hear you." I stood up and walked down to where I had my bike. I had no idea how I was going to do this, I didn't even know if I was good enough to try but I knew I couldn't leave her. I knew she would leave me one day and when she did my world would end but I wasn't going to be the one to leave her or our baby.

It took me longer than normal to get to the hospital. Every time I was close to getting there, I would just drive past my exit. I was being a pussy and I knew it. I was scared of the whole situation. I didn't know what she was going to say to me, or even if she was going to accept my apology. *What if she didn't want to keep the baby? That would be fine with me. But what if she did? Would she know that I would prefer not to?* That was usually a downer in a relationship, at least all the ones that I'd ever heard of. I already knew that I wanted her as my ol' lady but I had no ring or proposal. I just knew that this was what I wanted. *What did she want?* I had so many questions.

Three hours after I had left the clubhouse to come back to the hospital, I walked into the doors and back to the floor where I had left Keeley. The doctor ran up to me as soon as he saw me.

"Sir, have you heard from your wife?"

What the hell? Did she tell everyone that I had walked out on her?

"No, I haven't spoken with her since I left earlier." He looked stressed at my answer. "Is something the matter?"

"Yes, I would say so. Your wife disappeared from the floor and we've not been able to locate her. She took her clothes and belongings with her but she has not finished her course of medication. Also, the pregnancy is causing very high blood pressure, which if not controlled, could cause some serious complications to both her and your child."

I blinked, trying to absorb the information that he was giving to me.

She left? Why the fuck?

"Ok, thank you doc. I'm going to try the house, see if she's there. If she comes back here, can someone please let me know."

"Of course." He reached out his hand to shake mine before he turned to continue his work on the floor.

I hopped on my bike and raced over to Keeley's house. She could be there alone and in pain. I felt like even more of a dick for leaving her now.

I walked into the house and could hear Max whimpering in the living room. I ran in expecting to see the worst and it was. Keeley was laying on the couch, crying, big, nasty, gut wrenching sobs.

"Hey, hey. What's this shit?" I walked over to her and tried to raise her up from the couch. When fast as lightening her hand flew up and smacked me hard across the face.

"Get the fuck out of my house." Keeley sat up on the couch, staring daggers at me.

"No, I'm not leaving. We need to talk."

"Oh, now you want to have a fucking conversation? Now you want to listen to me?" More tears streamed down her face.

"Keeley, I fucked up-"

"No, you don't say?" She threw her hands on her hips as she stood up from the couch, wobbling a bit.

"Look, I know you are pissed-"

"Well, you got that right Dr. Obvious, I mean-"

"Are we going to fucking talk, or are you going to act like a raving bitch the whole time?"

I watched her whole face turn beet red and her eyes nearly pop out of the sockets.

Well, that wasn't the smartest thing to say right then.

I jumped behind the couch just before the first vase hit the wall right where my head had been. Books and glasses were being hurled in my direction, Max was barking and growling but she had given him no order to attack, yet.

"Bitch? You think I am acting like a bitch? I'll show you, bitch!" A plate came swirling through the air crashing against the wall and the shattered pieces bouncing back towards me. I covered my eyes, but a few pieces flew in just the right angle to slice my cheek and forearms. The blood infuriated me.

"How the fuck could you do this, Dillon? You made me love you then you left me!" Another book flew in my direction.

I could hear her breathing heavy, she was getting tired and I suddenly remembered what the doctor said about high blood pressure. All this screaming and throwing shit couldn't be good for her or the baby. Now I was more concerned for them then I was for myself. They couldn't be hurt, not because I was a coward.

I jumped over the sofa right as she was going to throw another glass figurine and I was able to bat it down as she let it go hurling through the air.

"You fucking asshole!" She screeched out at me. I saw her reach down and pick up another book, but I was on her quicker than she could've imagined. I had her pinned to the wall. Her face to the paint and her ass to me.

"Stop the shit, Keeley. I shouldn't have said that. It was wrong."

"Wrong! You leave me to deal with all this shit and then you come in here and call me a bitch and you say it was just wrong."

She was struggling against my hold, fighting to get free and get a weapon to beat the shit out of me. I had never seen her this angry. My little snake was spitting venom, and I was just trying to make sure I didn't get caught in the fire.

"Was this all a game to you? Did you want to see how far you could take it with me? Now that you know, you want to bail out?"

I pressed down harder on her, she was kicking and clawing at me but all I could really feel was her ass rubbing against my cock. I knew it wasn't the right time to be thinking about that, but the way she was fighting and screaming at me was turning me on. My woman was no weakling, not by a long shot. She would fight until the end and I loved that about her.

She must have felt my dick getting hard because she stopped fighting so much. "Is that all you wanted from me, pussy?"

"No, you know better than that Princess. I can get pussy from whoever I want."

The struggling started again but I held fast. "I don't want no one else but you."

"You're a fucking liar. You were just using me! Fine! If this is all you want, take it!"

What? What is she talking about now?

She spun around in my grasp, her heated eyes now staring into mine, no longer full of tears. *Much better.*

"Keeley, stop the nonsense. That's not what I want right now." I still had one hand in my grasp but the other one was no longer pinned to the wall, so she used it to grab my dick. Hard.

"Liar," she growled out at me.

I made no sudden movements. If there was one thing, I had learned with women, it was don't argue with an angry woman when they have your dick in their hands.

"No, this is what you want." She moved her hand from my dick to unfasten her sweatpants. They fell and she was naked underneath. I was fighting myself not to take advantage of her right now. She wasn't in her right mind.

"Keeley, stop right now. I don't want to hurt you. Stop."

"Too late, you weren't thinking about not hurting me when you walked out of that room." She went to unbuckle my pants, and I let go of her hand to stop the other one. She smacked me again, hard across the face. I had to take that hand and grab the swinging arm, which allowed her to use the free hand to undo my pants and get my cock out. My other hand was keeping her pressed against the wall so she wouldn't have enough space to raise a leg to kick me. I was hard as steel, hot and pulsing already in her hand.

"I told you, you're a fucking liar. All I was to you was a quick fuck. Was I good?" She began to pump her hand on my cock, hard and fast. She used the precum she squeezed from the tip to lubricate my shaft. "Was I the best? Is that why you kept coming back?"

"Keeley, stop!" I hissed through my teeth. I tried not to get any pleasure out of what she was doing, but my body was being a traitor and I was letting up on her. She had more room to maneuver now. She raised her leg, resting her foot on a ledge by the fireplace we were standing next to. She arched her body in such a way that she was able to rub her honey pot with my length, back and forth, a tease. Never letting me in but just letting me feel how wet and warm she was.

"Tell me the truth, for once in your life. Was I better than average?"

My eyes rolled back into my head. It felt so good. The friction of her clit and pussy lips against the tight skin of my cock had me going out of my mind. My hips began to buck forward without my conscious permission.

"Keeley, please... don't make us like this... don't do this." My hand dropped from holding her wrist up to gripping ferociously on her hip, trying to angle her up so I could get inside.

"Or maybe it wasn't my snatch at all, maybe it was my mouth?" She jammed both hands into my hair and yanked my head hard to her mouth. Her teeth smashed into mine before her tongue slid its way into my mouth. My whole body came alive. I could feel bliss rolling through every muscle that I had. I kissed her back hard and full of passion. I could feel her anger, but I could also feel the love. She loved me; I knew it.

I was still pumping against her honey hole, the tease of the whole situation was enough to have me humping her thigh like a dog in heat, and that tease along with the kiss and just the feel of Keeley back in my arms was enough to bring me to the edge. I held back though. I was sweating from mere exertion and the once irate Keeley was now mewling and panting against me. I felt her body start to tense, and very subtly she shifted her pelvis upward so the very crown of my cock entered her sweet spot.

Sparks and flashes of light collided behind my eyelids, as I threw my head back and roared up towards the ceiling. I nearly lifted off the ground, trying to get deeper inside her. I couldn't hold back anymore.

I grabbed her other leg off the ground, wrapping them both around my waist, not bothering to ask if she was ready. With one deep growl, I rammed into her as hard as I could. All ten inches of me from head to base straight up into her. Her eyes went wide, and her hands shot back to mantle above her head as she tried to pull herself away.

Too deep, too fast.

I have had plenty of girls tap out after I did this to them. I had learned from an early age since I was so blessed most girls had to get used to my length before I could go crazy. That was if they ever got used to it.

I stopped immediately. I watched her eyes as she settled back down on my rod. She loved it, but she wasn't looking at me the same. She was angry.

I reached up and caressed her face, no reaction, instead Keeley closed her eyes and started to move her hips. She was fucking me.

No, not this time.

I grabbed her hips hard and kissed her cheeks softly. I ran my fingers down her face. I was going to lose her; I could feel it.

"I am so scared, Keeley." I had never admitted my fear to anyone ever. "I don't know what to do. I know you're scared too. I shouldn't have walked out when you needed me. I needed you then too. How can I keep you? How can I keep a baby safe? I don't know what to do." I sighed as I leaned my head into the crook of her neck. I didn't want to look at her and see that hatred in her eyes anymore. I was deep inside her and she was in my arms, it felt like home. Something I'd never felt for any place besides the club before.

"I…" Her voice was a whisper but it was soft. I raised my head to look in her eyes. The tears were back but the anger was gone. "I can't do this on my own, Dillon, I can't. I know you're scared, but I have to trust that you're going to be my man and be by my side when things get rough, not run away." She ran her fingers down my face, and she kissed me again, gentler this time. I kissed her back.

"I'm yours. I'll never run from you. Never." I kissed her again, raising her small body up before slowly pulling her back down. I would never get my fill of this woman.

She let her head fall back as she fell further and further into bliss. "I'm yours too, Dillon. Only you." She moaned.

I picked up the pace. It had been so long. I tried to compose myself but I couldn't.

"Keeley, marry me. Be my ol' lady." I buried myself deep inside her. Her head snapped back up as she looked at me; her hips never stopped moving.

"Dillon, don't play with me."

"You going to make me beg, woman?" I pulled her back up, feeling her walls stretch and tremble around me. I dropped her back on me, could feel her body tensing up for her release. I let her upper back rest on the wall behind us while I leaned away from her, making sure I was in the right position to brush against her g-spot. I usually didn't need any extra tricks, but if this was a way to get her to say yes, I wasn't above cheating. I wanted her to agree.

"Oh... oh, oh..." Her eyes darted up to mine and her face scrunched a bit like she couldn't understand what I was doing to her body. Confusion. It wasn't until the quick and powerful burst of her orgasm had her back jerking off the wall did she realize she was cumming. She screamed my name as her body sucked at my cock. I kept up my monstrous pace, keeping the same angle. Before she could properly come down from her orgasmic high, she was cumming again. She pounded my chest with her hand and the only word I could understand from her high pitch screams was my name.

"Dillon!"

I felt her body go taut again and a high whimpering cry leave her mouth. She shook all over, and after a long second her pussy throbbed and sucked at me. I growled, using every muscle I had to force myself not to come. I wanted her to do it again.

"Oh, Jesus, I can't... Impossible." She was whimpering; her body limp against mine. She would fall straight to the floor if I let her go.

"You can't what?" I said through gritted teeth.

"Dillon!" She screamed my name again but didn't answer me.

"You can't what?"

"Orgasm, so many already... Can't..."

I felt an evil smile crawl up my face.

Challenge accepted.

"Give me one more," I whispered close to her ear.

Her shirt was plastered to her skin from the sweat pouring off both of us. I leaned down to kiss her, nibbling lips, inhaling her scent all while I kept up the excruciating pace.

"Dillon... Dillon.... oh my god..." Her body tensed up, her thighs wrapped around my waist shook with the force of an earthquake. I felt her pulse and suck at me, and finally, with a prayer to whichever god put this woman in my life, I let go of my seed inside her.

I grabbed her off the wall and let myself fall to my knees, making sure to cradle her against me as we collapsed to the floor.

"Yes." She mumbled against my chest.

"Yes?"

"I'll be your ol' lady."

I bent down the best I could, my insides were ecstatic but nothing but a slight smile on my face. Just before my lips could reach hers, she grabbed my cheeks tight in one hand.

"But if you run from me again, I swear on my life I will never cum for you again."

It took everything in me not to laugh in her face. I failed. I didn't have enough strength to stop it. The loud, raucous noise spilled out my lips as I laughed to the sky. I looked back down to her to see that she was frowning. She was serious. It only made me laugh harder. I could play that woman's body like a drum, she was going to have to come up with a better threat.

The budding smile on her face told me that she also knew what I knew to be true. She was all mine, anytime I wanted her.

"Jerk! You could at least pretend!" She slapped me lightly on the chest before she moved up and kissed me.

CHAPTER 26

Wire

I walked into the clubhouse the next morning with Keeley by my side. I had to be at the clubhouse to find out what was going on with the Tears, but I wasn't about to let her stay out of my hands for long. I had finally convinced her to stay with me at the clubhouse for a little while until things calmed down.

Really I just felt a lot better with the club doctor on standby. She hadn't complained of anything and the one time they did take her blood pressure, it was only a little bit elevated.

"So, do you want to talk about this baby situation?"

I was expecting to feel a sense of dread, but instead, I only had curiosity. "How did this happen?" I asked sincerely.

She smiled a little and in typical Keeley smart ass form said, "Well when a mommy and a daddy..."

"Ha...ha...ha, I'm serious, what about that IMTD thing?"

"The what?"

"The birth control thing."

She rolled her eyes slightly. "The IUD."

"Yeah whatever, the useless crap."

"I asked the doctor that as soon as you left. He said it seems the device moved or repositioned, making it ineffective."

"How do you move it?"

"I don't move it. Usually, you have to go to the doctor for it to be moved. I have heard stories about women who slept with well-endowed men..." She raised her eyebrows at me, glancing down to my package then back up to my face.

The caveman inside of me wanted to beat my chest. I was deep enough inside her that an object implanted there by her doctor had shifted out of place. I couldn't lie; I was a little impressed with myself.

"Does it hurt?"

"Being pregnant?"

I nodded once. I can't imagine that it was comfortable. "Actually, I had no idea. No morning sickness, no bloating, nothing. I don't think I would have figured anything out until my belly started to get bigger."

"How far are you?"

"The doctor said almost three months. So I'm almost out of the first trimester."

"Ok. What should I do?" I could feel the panic beginning to rise. I didn't know how to handle this, even talking about it was driving me up a wall.

She laughed and kissed me gently, immediately destressing me. "Nothing, Dillon. Just be here for me, get me ice cream and pickles, don't call me fat when I look like a whale in a few months, love me and love your baby. That's it."

"What if I don't love him right?"

"Him! Who said it was a him? What if it's a she?"

"Please, I am way too manly to be shooting chics. It's all testosterone here baby!" I rubbed her stomach lightly, watching her giggle as she put her hand over mine.

"There is no wrong way, Dillon. You're going to be a great father and a great husband. I can put money on it."

I hoped that she was right; I prayed that she was. I needed her to be right.

"Dillon, Dillon, wake up!" Keeley was beating me on my chest. We had just fallen asleep a few hours later and I was getting some really good sleep.

"No…" I grumbled and tried to turn around.

"Dillon, there's smoke!"

I finally heard the panic in her voice. My eyes popped open as I saw the smoke slowly seeping through under the door. I bolted up, put my feet in my boots and grabbed her, running for the door. She had on a pair of my sweats and a t-shirt. I could see that there was a fire coming from downstairs, but not one alarm had gone off. Everyone was still asleep.

"Keeley, get out of the building!" I pushed her towards the stairs.

"No! Come with me!"

"I have to wake them up! They're probably all drunk." Before I could say another word, she ran to the other side of the balcony and started banging on doors with all she had.

I ran over to Clean's room. Kicking it with my boots. "Clean, wake the fuck up! Clean."

"Fuck off!" I heard him scream back.

"Fire, man! Get out of the room!"

"Bullshit." I heard the bed creak; he'd turned over. I banged again, furiously on his door. "Clean, this is not a fucking game. The club is on fire, get the fuck out now!"

Within a second, he swung the door open. He had so much junk on his floor that the smoke couldn't even make its way in under the door crack.

"Oh shit!" He dove back into his room and grabbed some pants and his boots.

I ran to the next door. Banging and screaming fire along the way. Less than two minutes later, whoever was in the building was out of their rooms and rushing down the stairs.

"What the fuck? Why didn't the alarms go off?" Prez called out as we made our way quickly down the stairs. Keeley was beginning to cough; the smoke was getting bad.

"I don't know!"

"Prez, the door is on fire!"

I turned to see the rest of the folks that were here with their hands over their faces. They couldn't breathe. And the doors were what was on fire.

There was only one door to the outside that seemed to be unscathed, so of course people ran straight for it.

"It's a trap!" I screamed, grabbing for Keeley, dragging her behind

WIRE: A WINGS OF DIABLO MC NOVEL

a table and down to the floor away from the smoke. Before I could get anyone else's attention, the shots began to ring out. People were being mowed down as they ran toward safety.

I could hear the screaming and the bodies falling to the floor, but I couldn't move off Keeley, I had to make sure she and the baby were not in the line of fire.

"What the shit?" I heard Clean yell out. I turned my head to see him also down on the floor behind a piece of furniture. Archer and Prez were in the immediate area.

"Wire! Get the guns from behind the bar!" Prez yelled out for me.

"Yeah Wire! Get the guns, boy!"

I put my head down. I knew that voice. Monte. He finally made his move. Smart really, the whole club was scattered around the town, and no one was going to come looking for him right now. We spent so long getting prepared and watching who he was going to recruit that we weren't prepared at home.

I moved to the bar on my belly, slithering like a snake. I could hear Monte laugh as the bullets rained down near me. He was a bad shot, thankfully.

I picked up a few six-shooters and the shotgun, it was all we had. I slid the shotgun to Clean since he was the closest and the others to Archer and Prez. I could see at least a dozen people out the door just waiting for us to start running towards them. It would happen, the smoke was becoming oppressive. Keeley was crying.

"We have to run for the door," I called out to Prez.

"It's suicide," he yelled back.

"Either way, it's suicide," Clean yelled back.

Archer coughed a few times, wiping the soot from his face. "He's right. We won't make it either way, and I don't want to burn to death."

I turned back to Keeley, who was still coughing and crying on the floor.

"Listen to me, this is going to be bad, you run and get out of here. You fight as hard and as long as you can. You and this baby have to be alright. Promise me!"

"We will be!" She screamed back.

I stood up and let the numbness take over my body for what I was sure was to be the last time. I fired towards the door determined to take as many of them out as I could, even if it was only to make sure Keeley made it out.

I could see the sparks of flash from the muzzles of the guns next to me but it wasn't until I noticed shots coming from behind me that I turned to see who it was.

A tall, older man, blond hair and tattoos going up his neck ran up to me. I raised my gun to his face but didn't pull the trigger. In that split second there was something about him that I recognized.

His eyes!

He had gold shimmering eyes, exactly like the eyes I loved. This was Marko Juric.

"Where's my daughter?" He yelled in my direction, his European accent almost too thick for me to understand what he was saying.

"We're all clear!" Another one of the people that had broken in through the back and saved our asses bellowed from near the door. I ran back to where Keeley was and picked her up from the floor. Her eyes went wide when she saw who was standing in the middle of the floor.

"Tata!" She screamed as I ran past him and out of the still smoking clubhouse, running over the bodies that both the Wings of Diablo and her father put down.

Everyone made it outside. All the club members went to work then, using the outdoor water pump to get the fire under control. The last thing we needed was a bunch of cops and firefighters sniffing around.

"*Idi pomoći,*" Marko yelled out to the four men that were surrounding him and Keeley. They were almost military-like. I assumed he told them to help out because they almost instantaneously began grabbing buckets of water and whatever else they could to help us put out the fire.

I looked over to Keeley. She smiled at me, giving me a thumbs up and took her father's hand and started walking.

She was ok. I couldn't believe we came through all of that together and alive.

CHAPTER 27

Keeley

I watched as Dillon grabbed the hose and began to spray the water to get the fire under control. Lucky for us, only the doors and a few other structures were wood, so even though the fires were burning hot and long, the majority of the building was still in good shape.

"What look is that, my daughter?" My father was standing right beside me for the first time in years, and instead of being upset, I couldn't have been happier to see him. I didn't know if it was the baby or because I was really just a daddy's girl at heart.

I reached up and threaded my arm through his and began to walk with him. We would always take walks and talk to each other.

"Tata, what are you doing here?"

"I heard messages from people. I wanted to make sure you were ok."

"What kind of messages?"

"Messages that someone was trying to kill my baby girl. I know you want to live life, but no one disrespects my family."

"I understand." It was always about respect for him. Never anything else.

"Key, look at me."

I looked back at my father. "Yes?"

"You know if anything ever happened to you, I would lose my mind, right?"

I had to stop walking at that. I knew he loved me, but he had never said it. Tata only ever talked about respect.

"Really?"

"Yes, after your mother, you are the only link to my heart and soul. I worked hard to make sure you were always safe that you wanted for nothing. Yes, I did it in strange ways, but I got the job done. So, when they told me that you had been in the hospital twice." He glared down at me hard, letting me know that he was disappointed. "I came over as soon as I could to make sure you were ok. And to kill whoever dared harm you."

I turned to look back at Dillon, who was still working hard. "You don't have to worry about that. Dillon took care of them already."

"Dillon? Who is this, Dillon? You like him?"

"I love him, Tata," I said.

"He isn't one of the family. People are waiting on you at home."

"He is my family. I want him. No one else." I sucked in a deep breath, ready to tell him the secret. "He is your family too." I dropped my hand down to my stomach, caressing it gently.

My father looked down at what I was doing, confused at first, then his eyes lit up. A tear threatened to fall. I'd never seen him cry.

"Beba?"

"Yes, Tata. I'm having a baby." I smiled wide so he could see that I was happy about it.

"Oh, Keeley!" He began laughing and locked me in a hug, picking me up off the floor and spinning me around.

I had no choice but to laugh too. I'd never expected him to be so happy.

"I'm going to be a grandfather? A papa."

"Yeah, also, Dillon and I are going to get married."

The laughter stopped, and quickly anger took its place. "He didn't ask."

"He asked me already, Tata," I was confused.

"He didn't ask me!"

Crap. I had forgotten about that little tidbit. A big respect issue there. You always ask the father for the daughter's hand in marriage. I had to get him out of this one, or my father may have him whacked.

"Well, it wasn't a real proposal. Dillion just let me know that he wants to, and I let him know that I want to. That's all, Tata. Of course, he will ask you first."

"He better." He grabbed my hand again, put it back in the crook of his elbow, and we continued our walk.

He told me about everything that was going on back in our country and how he was essentially just in the background now and that he was as tired of all the fighting as I was. He was adamant that he would buy a home here in the states now so that he could be closer to his grandchild. He wanted to be a part of everything.

I apologized for how I left and he apologized for not believing in the work that I wanted to do. He said he would try to be more understanding about it even though he didn't see the need for it.

We walked back to the front of the clubhouse and I could see Dillon and the rest of the Wings of Diablo that were in attendance were already going through the dead, the fire done and taken care of.

Dad let go of my arm and pushed me gently towards Dillon. "Tell that boy to come over here so I can talk to him man to man."

I gulped down the fear that began to rise in my throat. My father would shoot Dillon in the face and not think twice about it if he thought that he was the wrong one for me. I hope he would be able to control himself.

CHAPTER 28

Wire

"Prez come look at this!" I called out as I turned over Monte's body. He was already starting to get cold. It was over, finally. Prez walked over and looked at the bullet hole dead center between Monte's eyes. Dead fucking center. Only one person here made that shot.

"Archer! Come see your handy work," Prez called over his shoulder.

I felt Archer walk behind me, he looked down at Monte. "Good, I'm glad he's out of the picture."

"Me too, but you couldn't do this shit before, could you?" We both laughed lightly until we heard Clean.

"Oh shit!" He exclaimed as he bent down to see someone else who'd been shot. I hated when Clean said *Oh shit*. Something was always going down when he did.

Prez and I walked over to where he was kneeling only to see him looking down at a dead Gin. It wasn't until I saw what he was wearing that I realized why Clean had said Oh shit. Gin was patched as a Tears of Chaos VP. I couldn't believe this shit; he'd been a traitor. He went against the family to our enemy. All those years we looked after each other's back. To know that he died trying to kill us? I spat directly in his face before I flipped his body back over roughly.

Fucking traitor!

That's how the Tears always knew what we were doing and who was where. They had a man on the inside who gave us the wrong information, so they could start a war. I couldn't understand why he would do this.

Prez sighed as he stood up from where he was looking at the patches on Gin's new kutte.

"How do you figure that?" I walked up to him, wanting to know the information.

"Gin heard the other higher-ups and me talking about promoting you, this was months back. Gin confronted me about it, saying that he was more senior, so he believed that he should be the one promoted. I said that you'd paid way more dues than he had." He looked back down to the body. "I just assumed that he let it go, guess he was upset we chose you over him."

"That's why? I would never turn my back on my family. Never."

"I hope you mean that for all of us," Keeley said from behind me.

I turned and grabbed her, trying to bring her in for a kiss. I wanted to feel her against me, feel that she was truly ok. She put her hands out, quickly stopping me. Fear evident in her eyes. *Since when was she scared of me?*

"What the hell is this, why can't I kiss you now?"

"You have to go talk to my Pops, Dillon. Don't think he wants to see you sucking face with his daughter."

I had to laugh a little. She was still scared of Daddy after all the things we had done together. Really?

"Don't laugh at me, Dillon. You have to go over there and ask him for permission about what we talked about earlier."

"Really?" Clean jumped in the conversation. "Y'all getting hitched?" He jumped in the air for a second before catching me in a bear hug and clapping me on the back. Archer and Prez were happy for me as well.

"Stop fucking celebrating. Are you crazy!" Keeley ripped Clean's hands off me, "You have to go ask first. I told him it wasn't legit, and that you were respectful.

"What the fuck for? I already asked, you already said yes."

"Bro, I would do what she says. That's not a man you want to disrespect."

"Yeah, why is that?" I asked turning to Archer since he had so much to say.

"Well for starters, that's Marko Juric, you know the head of the

Croatian Mob? Also, I heard he keeps heads in the closet of people that disrespected him. So, there's that."

My mouth dropped open.

He's a fucking mob boss! Holy Shit!

Even as a badass biker, we all know one group not to fuck with under any circumstance, was the mob. Here I was about to marry into one.

"A mob boss?" I turned to Keeley, suddenly starting to feel a little nervous.

"Yes, that's why I left. I was tired of the killing, but he isn't going to let me marry you if he thinks you aren't worthy. I already told him that we love each other and that you're a good man who can protect me, but you have to go in there and make him believe it." She stood behind me and pushed me towards her father, who was standing between four men in suits. You would never guess they had just been in a gunfight or fighting a fire. They stared me down as I made my way towards Marko.

"Leave us."

It was all he said, and they turned in almost a synchronized fashion, leaving Marko and me alone to talk.

I am so fucked.

"Keeley says that you got her pregnant."

"Yes, she's carrying my child."

"Is that what you do in this country, just knock up random women? Have you no control over yourself?"

I felt myself getting agitated already. Keeley wasn't a random woman; she was my everything. I had to let the anger go. He didn't know that yet. "Yes. I do have self-control. We thought that she couldn't get pregnant, that we were both safe."

"You going to take care of the beba?"

"Of course and Keeley. She's my world."

"You think so until you have to choose between this club and her, then you will leave her to do the bidding of your men. It always happens. It's how her mother grew to hate me." He looked away.

"I will never leave my brothers and she knows that, but I want her to be my woman. She holds more than just my seed; she holds my very soul. I wouldn't be half the man that I could ever be if she were to leave me, and my brothers know that. They know I need her and she knows I need them. We are a family."

"You are going to keep her safe?"

"With every breath in my body."

He smiled and put an arm around my shoulder. "You'd better because if I hear different, I'll come over and grind you up for a nice stew." He clapped me once on the shoulder before letting me go.

"Sir, does that mean I can marry your daughter?"

He turned back towards me. "Da! Get her a big ring. The Princess deserves the best!" He smiled as he turned away to walk towards his daughter.

Clean and Archer started whooping and hollering in the air when they saw that I wasn't dead and her father was smiling, coming toward them. They knew that my life had just changed, that my family had just officially gotten bigger. I couldn't be happier.

EPILOGUE

WIRE

I took off the suit jacket and threw on my kutte. Keeley and I had a massive wedding. At least four hundred people showed up, most of them from some European country to show respect to her father. They stuffed money in our hands and wished us luck in our life together. Keeley was already almost seven months pregnant, so she was really tired from all the activity, but we still had one more part of the day to go through. She had to be inducted into the club as my ol' lady.

I walked out of Clean's room, trying hard not to trip over the trash that was threatening to swallow up every inch of the room and saw my woman walking down the stairs on the other side. She had a pair of tight jeans on, riding boots and wife beater. It was tight around her round belly, and that only made it sexier.

I made my way down the stairs before her and held out my hand as she joined me in front of Prez and the rest of the higher-ups.

"I call to order today a club church meeting. We have matters to discuss." Everyone hooted and hollered.

"Wire, you have shown nothing but good judgment your entire life with us. You are a true definition of a brother, exactly what the Wings of Diablo strive to be. Now you come to us and ask that Keeley, aka Princess, be inducted into our family?"

"I do," I said loud and proud. I wanted everyone to hear that I wanted this woman, that she was mine.

"Princess, do you swear to uphold our laws and protect this club, before anyone else?"

She replied, "I do."

"Do you realize that this life is not for the weak or the unsure. There is no leaving once you are in."

Again she replied, "I do."

"Does anyone have any reason she shouldn't be accepted as our family."

The entire club exploded in an uproar, applause, and hollering, showing Keeley their acceptance into the family. In their hearts and minds, she was already one of us.

"So be it!" Prez had to scream above the noise. "Wire, claim your woman."

I took out the chain that was hanging out my pocket and slipped it over her head. It was a platinum chain with a small pendant of our logo and my name etched in. She would never take this off, and everyone who saw it would know that she was mine. I was never giving her up. She kissed me quickly once as everyone else descended on her, the other ol' ladies. The higher-ups, everyone in the club accepted her with open arms.

The night drew on, and the party in our honor was in full swing, strippers and bike bunnies were all over the place, and the music was blaring. Everyone was having a great time. I saw Keeley sitting at the bar, staring at me.

She must be tired.

I walked over to her, putting my beer down on the bar. "You ready to get some sleep?" I asked, leaning close to her ear.

She reached down to my cock and rubbed it through my pants. I hissed at the contact. I wasn't expecting her to be needing me.

"We got all our life to sleep. Right now, take me upstairs and make me scream."

I inhaled, growling into her neck. I would never get tired of this woman. I picked her up, making sure not to put too much pressure on the baby bump and hot-footed it toward my room. The loud echoing applause behind us let me know my brothers knew exactly what was about to happen. I was going to get some really good sleep tonight!

THE END

Find out more about the Wings of Diablo MC in Book 2, Archer!

YOUR SNEAK PEAK OF ARCHER!

Chapter 1

Pump, pump, pump it up!

"That's what I'm talking about!" Clean began to shimmy next to me, apparently, Joe Budden's music was his jam.

"Stop the shit! Get your head in the game, we have a job to do here." Wire spat out.

"You're right, I'm good." Clean stood up straight not wanting to piss our Vice President off.

I didn't really think that was possible, Clean was Wire's best friend even if they'd never told each other how they felt. Wire would do anything for him and vice versa. Actually, I'm sure anyone in the crew would do anything for any member. It's why I'm here today. No one messed with the Wings of Diablo, not if they wanted to live a long and healthy life.

Larry, one of our oldest members, came to the club with a problem that not many could solve. His sister had been sold off like cattle to the highest bidder by Cleve, the leader of one of our rival motorcycle clubs, The Rolling Cobras.

The Cobras were as bad as they came, heavy in the drug scene, hired guns and now they were dabbling in the human trafficking business. We knew as soon as Larry told us that Cleve would have to be eliminated, with fucking pleasure. There was no way we were going to let that go down. Not to Larry, not to his sister and not in this town.

"Ok, Archer, it's your show now, where do you need to be?" Wire turned toward me. His eyes staring straight into mine. The monster that so many were afraid of so clearly about to break free.

"The higher the better, maybe up there on the second floor if we can get up there."

Cleve was well guarded; we couldn't get to him using Wire and his sadistic ways. Prez would never come near here as the Cobras would probably shoot him before he stepped foot in their clubhouse, I had to be the one to take him out, something I anticipated.

"Hurry the fuck up!" Wire whisper-yelled at me.

"You can't rush perfection."

"God damn, gunnys! Just set up and take the fucking shot. We're going to be spotted any second."

As much as I did want to take my time and do the job smoothly, Wire was absolutely right. Intel said that there was going to be a party tonight, so we thought that would be the best time to sneak in undetected, but this wasn't just a party. No, the Cobras were throwing a goddamn full-blown event. There were hundreds of people here, the place was packed with strippers, bikers, college kids, and even fucking contortionists. Clean got a kick out of watching them bend and twist for the few seconds that we could. That many bodies would make my job that much harder and we risked someone spotting us by accident, we could only hope that it wouldn't be someone who would know who we were.

"Are you ready yet?" Clean whispered from beside me. He was crouched down looking back toward the stairs that we had just come up.

"Yeah, get ready to run." I laid down on the floor, one hand on the grip my finger laying against the trigger guard. The other hand was folded tightly underneath the grip to give extra stability, my eye open and staring down the scope of my M2010 rifle.

I exhaled slowly and just as I was about to squeeze the trigger a tingle flew down my back.

"This is fucked, Wire, there are too many people here. The target is too motherfucking tight." Removing my eye from the scope, I shook my head.

"Archer, can you pull this off or not? We are only here because you said that you could make this shot. We don't have time for fucking games!"

"Don't question my damn skill, I have made this shot a hundred times over. Just never in the middle of a fucking party." I exhaled roughly through my nose. He had no idea how easy it would be for me to make a shot like this; no idea whatsoever.

"I know you're skilled brother, but if you don't think we should do this we have to get out of here, pronto. If we get caught on enemy territory there's no telling what they will do."

Wire was our clubs Vice President as well as its enforcer, his specialty was with barbed wire, something he favored when he tortured people. He knew what would happen if we got caught here and so did I.

"So what's the deal, maybe I can sneak one of those bunnies out of here." Clean looked across the room to one of the strippers, who was in the middle of doing some truly acrobatic shit on a pole.

"Keep your dick in your pants, Clean."

"Oh, I'll keep it in but she might want to take it out." He smiled a little still staring at the woman.

"Are you fucking dense, we're lying here with a motherfucking sniper rifle pointed at the president of a vicious, murderous motorcycle club and all you can think about is getting your dick wet?" I stared daggers at Clean, and by the way his jovial face fell and became somber I could tell that he got my message. This was not a game, we were in some serious shit.

I hunkered down into position, my eye back to the scope, staring straight at my target. I sucked in a deep breath slowly and held the rifle steady, waiting for the perfect opportunity when the target was clear. I didn't want any innocents walking into the line of fire. Exhaling slowly, I gently squeezed the trigger, sending the bullet on its destructive mission.

"Oh shit," Clean said at my side.

Before the ripple that crept up my arm from the recoil could finish, I knew the shot was fucked. I watched as Cleve went down, but also a petite woman who happened to be standing right behind him.

Not only did I hit my target, but the bullet sailed clean through him.

Make sure you download book 2 of the Wings of Diablo MC, Archer here!

NEXT UP IN WINGS OF DIABLO

Get your copy here!

Blurb:

Archer-

I am the master marksman at the Wings of Diablo MC Club. Any target my brothers need me to take down, I will. I am a magician with a firearm no matter the class, from the small and simple Glock 36 to the powerful .44 Magnum, the big bad shotgun to the sleek and sexy M2010. I have been known to be stoic and calculated. To lay above the rest and smile as each bullet sailed through my target. Once you were in my sights, you go down for the long nap. I used to believe that my fate was sealed by the bullet and my gun, come to find out my life would be turned on its head by Daria. A woman in the wrong place at the wrong time. A woman who is seared into my soul.

Daria-

My whole life I stayed to myself, never wanted to get anyone upset or be a burden to those around me. So when my roommates strong arm me into going to a party at the Rolling Cobras MC Clubhouse I try to stay as far away from the action as possible. Not that it did me any good, my favorite shirt was ruined, I got hit on by a man missing his two front teeth, oh and I got shot in the chest. Talk about a party. There was one good thing that came from that horrible experience, the hospital set up a trauma counselor, Archer. There is something about his haunted eyes that makes me believe that I can trust again. No one makes my pulse race like he does, makes my body surrender like he does. Even with secrets all around him, I have no choice but to submit to him.

MORE FROM RAE B. LAKE

Wings of Diablo MC
Wire
Archer
Clean
Cherry
Prez
Ryder
Ink
Roth
Mack
Storm

Wings Of Diablo MC - New Orleans
Jameson
Yang

Spawns of Chaos MC
Shepard

Juric Crime Family

Sven's Mark

Eve's Fury MC
Becoming Vexx
Free
Riot

The Shop Series Books
His Georgia Peach
To Protect and Serve Donut Holes
On The Edge of Ecstasy
His Peach Sparkle

Royal Bastards MC
Death & Paradise

Standalones
Drunk Love
Saving Valentine

FOLLOW RAE EVERYWHERE!

FACEBOOK
READER GROUP
TWITTER
INSTAGRAM
GOODREADS
AMAZON
WEBSITE
BOOKBUB
NEWSLETTER